I Can't Believe This!

A Collection of Humorous

New & Classic

Short Stories

BY

CAROL COOK

Cover design: Carol & Bob Cook and Print One

ISBN#: 978-1-7328019-2-9

Printed by Amazon/Carol Cook/ US

DEDICATION

To Carol Cook

I've been through so many happy

and crappy events and several

brushes with the end that I believe

seven of my nine lives*

have been used.

Therefore, this book is for my self

*Celestial sign - Lion

Humor is emotional chaos remembered in tranquility.

\- James Thurber

Table of Contents I

Table of Contents - II

Introduction

For decades Carol has complained, protested, and documented the behavior of everyday people, those who crossed her path and some who simply conducted themselves in rather odd practices. She has observed, questioned, and celebrated the quirky situations and failings the general population finds themselves in, creates, and participates in. She reveals the interesting, haphazard, and frustrating antics of modern life in frank conversations that leave us shaking our head in amazement. Chronicling accounts of the confused and hilarious life we live, the products we use, and the outcome of spouting words without thought.

In her intimate and charming voice Carol's short stories and essays speak to us candidly on the lapse of judgement in so many that we feel skeptical and curious over these deeds committed by those we thought of as the smartest citizens among us. Her uproariously funny and truthful takes on daily misgivings by sensible-appearing people and her jarring honesty on news reporters spouting twisted, fake accounts of everyday happenings leave us challenged and give us pause for thought. Why we ask are so many twisting the truth, finding themselves in places they shouldn't be, and behaving as if they have little respect for anything? Just as scary, why is our government lying to us constantly?

With hints of sarcasm she shares her sentiments on laundry, the art of talking, heaven, and toilet tissue. Offering laugh-out-loud straight up talk on our lawns, mosquitoes, and how luggage became a fashion accessory. She asks if the lack of commonsense in so many will be ongoing to the point intelligent life on other planets may look at Earthlings as the most foolish bunch of nincompoops in the universe. Carol suspects they're asking about the younger generation of Earth too, wondering if they will ever wise up and stop replying, "I have no idea"!

Commonsense isn't common - Voltaire

I Can't Believe This!

This is unbelievable. Of all the phony, ridiculous crap I've read over the years, this takes the cake. Why this would be considered worthy of reporting is baffling. However, it appears the research scientists with Procter & Gamble, one of the largest makers of cleaning products, spent a great deal of time looking into this while the world was confined, honestly believe their research is important, but it has truly created a headshaking moment.

Personally, as a housework hater, procrastinator is a better description, this sounds like a marketing ploy, a hoax to increase product sales for P & G. It appears they are attempting to convince consumers they should enjoy cleaning, doing the laundry, and more when it comes to keeping a home or business sanitized, free of germs, dirt, and livable.

This is just puzzling. P&G sought out behavioral psychologists to study how those saddled with cleaning can feel good, elated over ongoing chores. The goal is to help the worker find a calming feeling, give a sense of accomplishment, and be relaxed and relieved knowing the task is finished, the job is done. Oh please.

The company wants to persuade consumers to associate cleaning with positive emotional breaks, think of the chore as finding your Zen using cleaning as a path to mindfulness. I'm not kidding, this is from the study. Cleaning can be the road to enlightenment, steer us past worries by meditating while cleaning. They want us to look at cleaning as an exercise in doing something in the present, use the experience of cleaning to keep an open mind, a stay in the moment of utopia rather than thinking of the chore as work they tell us. Who would fall for this?

Their research hopes to convince us to feel good about cleaning, take pleasure in the task of keeping our spaces whistle clean. Seriously, they are telling us to clean and freshen up a little every day instead of letting it build up. And while we launder and disinfect, we're to believe the chore is rewarding, and we'll find solace in it. I don't think so!

Who in their right mind wants to clean every day? You won't believe this either; P & G scientists have made an app to teach us how to clean and feel excited, turn the chore into a thoughtful and therapeutic project. Cleaning can give us a foothold of control, be in tune with daily sprucing up, and give us a sense of selfless accomplishment, so says the meditation leader. Seriously! What do they expect us to do, dance around the room with a mop and broom?

To some this may sound like a ploy to sway the consumer into thinking that cleaning products are a gift to mankind. The psychologists tell us by following their guidelines, we will experience feelings of mindfulness and a sensation of radiance about us! Then they add we may experience vibrations of bliss and joy if we will wash, scrub, scour, mop, wax and overall spend time cleaning everything in sight. I'm not kidding, these are the actual words from their study.

And, there's more. The app created instructs us to notice our breathing while washing dishes or moping a floor, feel the warmth of the water temperature and the smell of the soap for a calming experience. If we are doing the laundry take time to feel the texture of fabrics, observe colors and patterns, perceive how they feel, visioning them as a soothing sky, peaceful green meadows, the dawning of a morning. By quietly standing at the washer we can commune with our clothes!

The research experts also want to convince us if we stay committed to practicing mindful cleaning, we will have a healthier relationship with the washing machine, the laundry, vacuum cleaner, dishes, and cleaning products. Who wants that kind of a relationship? I don't care if they are scented with flowers and herbs; this is a bunch of hooey, only a recluse personality would have friendships like that!

I believe the behavioral psychologists need a life and have personally never had to spot clean mud, mustard, snot, formula spit up, or kid poop from the laundry. Nor have they ever had to scrub stains from the carpet when the dog threw up or had diarrhea because your five-year old shared part of a chocolate Easter bunny with the dog.

My personal take? Anyone who wants to clean every day most likely has a dirt and germ phobia and is a certified clean freak. The masses don't want relationships with the washing machine or cleaning products. We want to be out frolicking, seeking out adventure, playing sports, out boating, at the beach, camping, fishing, golfing, or the quiet of the mountains, time with loved ones and having fun living.

We've got ongoing happiness and trials to attend to, rapture and magic, and turning the ordinary and smallest events into memories and love. We're focused on living and believe in the Scarlett O'Hara outlook, tomorrow is another day, the cleaning can wait.

As the Cookie Crumbles

Betrayal, cheating, lies, and more in the form of shouting of accusations, foul play and misdeeds cited in the cookie community have been in the news recently. I'm serious, it's been reported on television and newspapers playing out like a soap opera. Complaints have been made with blame and pointed fingers directed at the number one cookie company in the world, Oreo Cookies. It's rocked the cookie business to the core and shocked consumers into disbelief.

The facts have been outlined in hearings, unsettling fussing, arguing, threats, and implication made against the cookie-making giant. The blame has been taken up by lawyers on both sides, investigations begun, and misconduct displayed before the truth finally came out. Experts and consumers asked why, surely this isn't true and what happened?

There are all sorts of stories swirling about, some don't pass the nose test, but it appears, unfortunately, part of the story is and is not true. And it seems, true to asking, it's always going to be something to sort out, most of us believe it may have been a stab at reality gone amiss. It was as if the moment your back was turned America's most beloved and popular cookie was slammed.

Why would the maker of this delicious, crunchy, cream filled, dark chocolate sandwich cookie be accused of dastardly deeds in store shelf wars? And is it true? Well, it seems the rival, cookie maker Hydrox Cookies, got rather upset, hopping mad actually, waging a fight against the worshiped Oreo cookie.

Oreo makers were accused of behaving like villains. "Poppycock", says the Oreo company to the charge they personally moved Hydrox Cookies to shelf areas consumers can't easily see. That's it. Hydrox Cookie has accused Oreo of hiding their cookie packages behind other packages of snack cookies causing sales to slump for Hydrox; this of course meant war.

This doesn't sound right, and who notices where cookies are located? Well, apparently, it's an issue for marketing they swear it matters where cookies are placed on the shelves. It really is a big deal, proven fact; certain placement on store shelves guarantees customers will see a product up front and center and buy them first if they immediately see the cookies. I'm not sure that's exactly true for wouldn't customers buy the cookie they love no matter where it's displayed?

It's entirely possible Hydrox doesn't have much of a case because their cookies simply aren't as popular as Hydrox thought they'd be. The facts are plain as day if truth be known, which is, their cookies just aren't as tasty as Oreos. Their cookies disappeared from stores in 2003 because of low sales, but they still didn't give up. Instead, the cookies were brought back in 2008 to stores with great gusto and a new marketing plan, unfortunately, sales once more crumbled.

Oreo continued its reign as the number one cookie for cookie lovers, bringing joy and solace across the land, life was good. But Hydrox refused to accept defeat and came up with a new plan again, bringing back their cookies to stores once more in 2015.

Apparently, the recipe wasn't changed, which meant their cookies still didn't taste heavenly chocolaty, good, so, sadly, sales stayed low. Could this possibly be the reasoning for a new fuss and new charges of aggressive and cruel tactics against Oreo makers? This sounds like a bunch of sore losers or the recipe for their cookie doesn't quite meet the standards and taste beyond the number one cookie on the planet, Oreo. Or is it possible there is a hint of jealously akin to a love/hate relationship making this saga a candidate for a soap opera drama?

Now we have the facts straight, its simple. Oreo cookie lovers are die-hard devotees, but to make sense of things a few Oreo cookie eaters tried the rival Hydrox but turned their back on what they deemed an Oreo-wanna-be. Millions across the world agree and believe Oreo is still and always will be the very best there is. Fortunately for Oreo, this cookie love/need has been passed down through generations from mothers and fathers to children and on to grandchildren.

All who love this delightful, yummy cookie agree its "saved many a day" when the need arises to satisfy a sugar craving, and more. The devotee of this beloved cookie truly knows it will fix what ails a body. The consumer of the number one cookie has experienced the wonder of its sugary taste and felt it immediately satisfy elevating their mood. Eating an Oreo cookie, or several brings on the happiest, most satisfying of feelings, awakens taste buds, and more. So, they reach for the crunchy chocolate, white crème filled Oreos to give a feeling of lasting joy and a bite of bliss that does more than satisfy hunger.

I'm serious; many stories are told after eating and enjoying this wonderful, beloved cookie. It has and will ease the hurt of a lost love, lost job, fend off the blues, or soothe a crying child. Oreo cookies have relieved great pain and loss, soothed the ache of failure, and the down and out let-downs from all sorts of calamities. But Oreo cookies have also been reached for to celebrate all sorts of happy times and events that are too many to list.

They have fixed wounded hearts, calmed the jolt of losing a football, basketball, baseball game, or a round of golf, even a scraped knee. They are famous for celebrating anything, winning, getting an award, a promotion, a new car, job, or home. Oreos satisfy the craving of a chocolate fix with just one or a bag full; the satisfaction is like nothing else. They delight and honor, praise and celebrate uncountable happenings, along with making parties and the end of a day rapturous.

Consider this too; if one looks in a thesaurus under cookie, Oreo is listed but there is no mention of Hydrox. Seriously, Oreo's rivals need to accept millions of devotees will never waver in their adoration. They will eat Oreo cookies forever, anytime, anywhere, for any reason, or float them in milk after scraping off the creamy white filling with their teeth, then swoon.

And why not? Treat yourself, indulge with the world's most satisfying cookie, or several, or the entire package, you only live once.

Baby It's Cold Outside

Getting through a winter predicted to be an icy-northerner, with a grip holding 'til spring, called for a warmer coat. Facing frigid, record-breaking temperatures meant replacing an older coat, (which never kept the cold and piercing, stinging winds from numbing the bones) was a necessity.

Discovering a going out of business sale meant a new, warm coat would be possible. True to expectations there it was, the perfect one. It was a steal on sale, a most delicious brown color with a tantalizing shine, soft as air, simply luxurious. I'd found a fur coat priced at barely more than an ordinary polyester blend and heaven knows polyester could never top the warmth of this enchanting wrap, nor offer the comfort of such a pleasant covering.

Discarding threats of fur protesters and attackers, warmth was needed; nestling into a pleasurable wrap offering protection from brutal wind and freezing sleet would be heavenly. Still, it seemed rather devil-may-care stepping into such a dare by wearing fur in a hostile animal rights activist era. But I did, reasoning the implications of a so-called moral misdeed felt delightfully warm.

As one of the first coverings used to survive, it's quite confusing how some can say we should not dress ourselves with fur during sub-freezing temperatures. It kept our ancestors from huddling around fire, and across the years fur kept generations alive, saving us from freezing to death before the furnace was invented. An extra bonus, animals the fur came from provided food for man to live.

You can't imagine the relief when my cousin gushed over my new coat, stating I must discard concern, possible rants from complaining activists; wear my coat with pride she instructed. "We, of American Indian heritage can wear fur, and feathers too if we choose", she added while slipping on my warm coat of fur.

It's true! Native Americans have wrapped themselves in fur for centuries when cold, harsh winters threatened to freeze man and beast. So, forget those who argue, pushing us to question our ethical outlook. The righteously concerned who shout, "Animals have rights", will always be here to remind us they disapprove of this and that, my cousin declared.

They rant and curse, point fingers, and condemn anything involving animals used to feed or clothe humans. "Wear it instead of goose down, which gives one a puffed-up appearance of the Michelin tire man trudging through the cold". "Besides, fur is so elegant", my cousin prattled on and on about the naysayers.

So, when this recent and surprising announcement appeared on the news, in medical journals, and on the Internet, I could have danced in celebration, rather like my Indian ancestor's ceremonial ones. A group of research doctors, scientists, and clothing manufacturers released a monumental statement; it moved fur haters and promoters of faux fur to slink away.

Faux fur products man created to replace animal fur as a fashion statement and appease critics, who charge wearing animal fur is immoral, abusive, and wrong, should listen up. Wearing faux fur made with chemicals and petroleum products has proven to bring on allergies and induce a variety of illnesses!

My fur coat is worn with a clear conscience during bitter arctic weather. When young grandchildren visit, they prance about wearing the coat playing dress up, pretending it's the Queen's robe. At bedtime, they fall asleep wrapped in a blanket of warm comfortable fur.

When I think of sneering pessimists shivering in the cold, moral rule makers disapproving of my coat of fur, I smile. The pleasure of its warmth and comfort kept me from feeling those teeth-chattering, frigid elements of winter. It's also given me memories of young grandchildren playing and laughing in their pretend fantasy world believing they wore and then slept wrapped in the Queen's robe.

Sizing It Up

Shopping is considered one of America's favorite pastimes, but let's define the difference between shopping and buying things. Shopping is a popular leisurely pastime for people the world over. Buying things is sometimes a chore, often confusing, more so today because manufacturers continually introduce newer, better, and bigger products.

However, there are times when buying necessities can be annoying and time-consuming, even boring when shopping for the same item's month after month, restocking what has been used up. Example: personal and household necessities that include hair products, toothpaste, laundry items, cleaning supplies, and toilet paper.

Why would an intimate item like toilet paper be brought up? Well, it was recently announced on national news there has been a big change to toilet paper rolls. We're told they aren't exactly what they used to be, actually, they've been transformed. Changed in such a way the new size is a tad surprising to consumers, which might give us pause for we imagine product researchers and marketing department heads may have gone too far.

Seriously, manufacturers too often perplex us with ongoing modifications to products, offering such an array of choices it can be frustrating at times. The newest product now available in toilet paper is huge, nearly the size of a go-cart wheel and weighing upwards of four pounds! Really, they named it the "Forever Roll", even though it really doesn't last forever. Although, with 1,700 sheets per roll it's reported to last three times longer than the regular double roll.

This newly introduced roll has created headlines, which has moved, no pun intended, larger families to shout out with enthusiasm; however, other consumers ask why. One reason, we're told the new giant size should only need replacing every three to four weeks. Of course, this depends on how many people are using it. If there are two or more teen-aged daughters in the house, or worse, the family cat unwinds the roll of tissue for self-amusement, the large roll would barely last a week.

This much we know is fact, searching for a suitable type of toilet paper does give one pause as options often overwhelm the best of shoppers when considering the following. Should I buy single or double rolls, one or two-ply, scented, unscented, ultra-soft, quilted, bio-degradable, environmentally friendly, recycled, septic safe, bamboo, or the luxury silk-touch triple-ply?

Confusing us more, we sort through at least a dozen brand names, which is rather perplexing. Angel Soft may have us ask, who knows how soft an Angel is? Charmin Ultra Soft and Northern Ultra Plush leave us with the question; which one is more, or less soft or ultra? Cottonelle Comfort Care puzzles us; what are we comforting, our behind or our psyche?

Adding to the bewilderment is the newest brand on the market, "Who Gives A Crap". I'm not kidding, this is really a brand; look it up. I'm sure it was created by a man because most men couldn't care less about toilet paper, they just buy the cheapest stuff.

Introducing the hefty forever roll will still have families arguing over who should replace the empty roll. Moms are usually in charge of the change out as most kids don't care if the roll of toilet paper is on the holder or sitting on the floor. Male occupants of a home often claim ignorance when it comes to replacing toilet paper. The most often used excuse; they don't know how to position it, install it to roll over or under?

Psychologists are giving opinions why some don't give a hoot about a bigger roll of toilet paper. Ordinary folks simply shake their head over the fuss because the only thing important; they just want it available and there, strong, and reliable.

Kind of like a super-hero.

The Crisis at Hand

Manicures have been a blessing for women since the beginning of civilized humanity. Cleopatra had her nails done every week; she chose to have them stained blood-red, which signified class. In China the royal men of the Ming dynasty used dyes to color their nails, while royal women chose to wear long fake nails to signify that they didn't do manual labor. Wish that worked for me.

For those who don't realize how important a woman's nails are to her should take this outline to heart. Well, it is documented proof. A woman's fingernails are one of her best assets, along with her hands and toenails. Keeping them manicured and feminine looking is pure joy and sinfully needed at least once a month, trust me.

This is amazing when I think about it. As a young woman I regularly spent time and money for manicures and pedicures because that's what girls did. We as females either do our nails our self or splurge and get them done at a salon. It's wonderful, a pleasure at hand, and the best of self-indulgence that elevates our mood to happy.

However, there was a time when my nails always seemed a mess, unpolished, broken, and uneven. I've been at war with them for years; not something I arrived at suddenly, it just sort of snuck up on me in little creeps and bits. Taking over my life was a new job, one that put me under the influence of small children, dust, and dirty dishes, laundry, and cleaning everything, constantly.

Over time, and something I had little of, my nails and hands began to look used, tired, and dull. They were not accustomed to confronting this new identity, the slow changing of life, the joys and sorrows of parenthood, the task of taking on housework and managing children.

It began with constant washing of everything in the house, bathing children, picking up toys, pulling bubblegum from rugs, days on end scrubbing spills, crayon marks, and food from the floors, furnishings, and walls. Cleaning everything in and out of the house on a daily basis took its toll on the appearance of my nails; a short time later it ambushed my psyche.

The battle to stay healthy and put-together looking by getting one's nails and toenails done seemed ongoing. There is work to be done at the office, repairs to mend at home, homework to supervise, grocery shopping, sports events to attend, sick kids to make well, and fusses among them to monitor. So, manicures sort of took a back seat to everything.

Time was spent finding anything in the dryer or in stacks of clothes to fit growing children or searching for a pair of shoes the dog had not chewed. Housewifery and mothering skills left little time to get a manicure, and occasionally had me asking; "Will I spend my entire life locked up in drudgery with broken, unsightly nails?

Seriously, these thoughts invade the minds of mothers daily. They become a fear, like being found out you flushed your child's dead goldfish, secretly replacing it with an identical live one. And so, the years passed, the recollection of beautiful, buffed nails and toenails became a foggy memory.

Un-kept, unpolished and un-manicured nails were the ultimate punishment, becoming part of my motherly appearance. They may have been responsible for a few clinically-paranoid, meltdown episodes over time, challenging me to set a goal as soon as the children were off to college or married, I would be free, and once again make those monthly nail appointments! Beautiful nails would become my signature; my emblem of life lived in luxury in my mature years.

The heart of the issue, lest anyone misunderstand me is that I've discovered women need to have perfectly manicured nails. That's right, it's a need. Seriously, the facts: We're more conscious of who and what is around us, we feel revived, able to solve problems which I'll not go into detail, but we can shop more professionally, and never feel a need to fool with those hokey sales either.

We tend to laugh more, enjoy a relaxing glass of wine for lunch with our best buds, and toss out all guilt over not getting the wash done that's piled up on the washer. Our nails have been done so why risk a chip or break. We're also a more tolerant group when our nails are buffed, polished to a signature color, and our toenails flashing a gleaming delightful color to match our lipstick and fingernails. Life is good.

Glamorous, painted nails are feminine and a luxurious grooming necessity, a present reality, a tradition. So, the advice here: Don't let laundry or cooking get in the way of a nail appointment under any circumstances. Women should never sink back to the feeling of having unkempt naked nails ever again. Seriously, keep that nail appointment, it makes life good.

The Fungus Among Us

To love and appreciate good food one has usually enjoyed it from the time of birth to adulthood. This means good food has been part of our upbringing, left us with a love for certain foods and great memories of some seriously good cooking. This of course describes myself, my family, and most of my friends.

So naturally I'm not exactly pleased about a report just out slamming good food, so I feel compelled to question who these research people are. Here are the facts. It seems the experts, and foodies have stepped right in the middle of the very thing that nourishes our body and soul, good, fortifying food. They don't appear fond of what we love to eat, which I find a serious issue because food scientists are messing with what we enjoy eating, challenging, and changing everything about it.

It appears the federal government has been sponsoring research for some twenty years to look into creating alternative food sources for an expanding world population. I didn't know this was going on and I bet most of the population didn't know it either. Now we have hundreds of strange products, new ideas, new directions, and odd stuff being used to produce fake food to replace the old standards. It's true, fake food!

This doesn't sound like what most of us believe should be, who among us wants to give up steak, burgers, bacon, potatoes, fried okra, macaroni and cheese, grits, fried chicken, and more? Unfortunately, researchers don't give a flip if we eat our beloved soul satisfying foods.

I'm not kidding. There are research people and experts that are determined to push alternative meat and vegetables on us. Their idea of alternative is new food made in labs using fermented mushrooms, mold, mildew, and DNA from plants and flowers, grass, weeds, and seeds, along with seaweed and other odd stuff they believe is healthier for us. Good grief!

It makes me wonder if they are adding dirt to this new, bogus food to try to fool us even more while touting it really does have a more natural taste. Their promise? The new foods being produced in labs will replace beef, pork, fish, and seafood, along with every vegetable they can imitate. The food geniuses are betting on fiber fungus-based proteins as the secret sauce to sway us into eating healthier, convince us not to eat and enjoy mashed potatoes and gravy, pinto beans and ham, cakes and pies. Can you believe this?

Research scientists have recently discovered an assortment of plants around the world that includes things from rain forests and organisms from remote mountain riverbeds to create mycelium, which is mold! They are attempting to convince us the new edible mold structure has lower fat content and savory amino acids that will produce a profile with high levels of fiber and protein.

They promise the new foods are much better for us and will replace not only every source of meat but every vegetable and dessert we love. Carrots, peas, squash, tomatoes, and other vegetables won't be the real thing anymore; they'll be created in labs with almost unspeakable ingredients. This doesn't sound good at all; why would they want to do that? Are we being conned?

The scientists are saying we need to find new foods to feed the growing world population and food grown in labs will solve this. The researchers promise this is healthier and has a more edible composition, low fat content and high levels of newly discovered infrastructures of micro-proteins they assure us support brain stability. What?

Well what about the icky taste that has been reported? They said they are working on this issue. Working on it, the taste is everything, but apparently not to them, they'll get to this later. The goal is to have various roots, algae, and fermented mushrooms and yeast as our answer to a healthier and longer life. Also, they've designated the new food of the future will save the world from hunger.

Even though reports have indicated people have become sick from eating these new mycelium's, the research is progressing. I don't care if they are making progress - who wants to eat fake food made from soil-based mold! And who knows where that came from, possibly scooped up from the moon for all we know!

Well, count me out! I'm not eating fermented mushrooms, mold and mildew to keep my brain stable and my figure slim! I don't care if weeds, tree bark, fungal organisms, dirt, and oxygenated liquids are low fat; I'm not into eating stuff that tastes and sounds terrible! Don't these people know chicken, fried steak, barbecue, mashed potatoes, gravy and biscuits, and pinto beans, cake and pie are a tonic, an antidote to whatever ails you?

Thank you to the worlds' entrepreneur scientists for trying to save the world but I'll cling to my fried chicken, barbecue, fresh fish, grilled burgers, French fries, and pie until I die.

The Green Grass of Home

A lush, green lawn shadowed with leafy trees, a spattering of scented flowers, and a place set aside for relaxing is paramount for homeowners. However, an eye-catching, well-maintained lawn takes planning, money, and work, often eroding leisure time. Still, hours of backbreaking labor are devoted to the task of achieving a masterpiece carpet of green.

The homeowner's quest for a groomed green lawn is the goal, a piece of beautiful real estate becomes a beloved domain. A lawn to enjoy, be proud of, work in, maintaining its appearance to keep it lush and immaculate, free of weeds, expertly edged and trimmed. It becomes a calming emerald retreat, nearly flawless, visually an unblemished place to relax and admire. Our haven that is almost too good to be true.

For some it isn't, the newest fad in lawns is fake. Yep, the new lawns and landscapes coveted by so many are artificial, a status symbol for homeowners, landscapers, and environmentalists. Lawns and the landscape surrounding some homes aren't real! That's right, we now manufacture fakes; man-made grass, plants, trees, artificial plants, and greenery of every kind being installed by landscape architects and designers to create perfection for outdoor areas. A homeowner's heaven with no work or upkeep is involved.

The new green synthetic grass gives us a no-maintenance, show-stopping, perfectly clean, faultless lawn; a brilliant maneuver for homeowners and their landscapers. The faux lawns are desirable, practical, and needed, especially in regions that are drought prone where water conservation is a must.

Being fake, the artificial outdoor space is available for use no matter the season; the negative? They're pricey. A 3,000 square foot installed imitation grass lawn will cost around $60,000.00. Add in artificial trees, plants, shrubs, the cost quickly escalates beyond $100,000. Not for the shoestring budget, but if one thinks rationally, it's a great deal.

Think about this. If costs for lawn upkeep, equipment, mowers and tools, fertilizer, plant food, tree trimming service, and ongoing maintenance hassles are added up, the fake lawn is worth every dollar. In addition, consider the benefits of no biting fire ants or slimy snails to step on, no marauding bugs and weeds taking over, no mowing or watering, it's a dream lawn.

The new green lawn is appealing to owners of small condos with tiny plots of outside space and to city dwellers with little sun, or those with terrace and rooftop areas. Faux grass, trees, and plants can be installed in settings once believed impossible, sometimes mixing in a few live plants and real stones to create the most welcoming, realistic, and relaxing retreat.

Other advantages of this modern-day marvel; no dirt or mud to track into the home, and a special place for Fido or Fluffy to go can be made available as well. Dogs and cats can have their own area as landscape designers have a solution with an under the turf water cleaning system and drainage area. Using a softer material with various green colors and blade lengths, it has a more natural like feel underfoot so pets believe its real grass.

This brings us to the point. No longer will homeowners face dilemmas achieving the perfect lawn. The faux outdoor space will eliminate hours of work and monitoring the health of everything growing. There will be no worry about property values falling because of an unkempt lawn. Nor will neighbors offer up shame because your lawn has become an eyesore. No arguments with a spouse over the lawn's shabby appearance will take place because weekends will be for playing, relaxing, and entertaining on your perfectly manicured faux lawn.

You might say this makes no sense for the lover of outdoor lawn care and gardening. They love what they are doing, need the exercise, the feel of outdoors, accomplishing something or growing anything. In any case, there are those who don't want to work constantly or endure the hassles of dirt, dust, bugs, and dead plants. So fake is a God-send, prayers are answered.

Could the trendsetting technology that is producing scientifically engineered lawns be the future? If so, will weekend nagging by a spouse be a thing of the past and will the grass still be greener no matter from which side we look?

Mosquito Blues

I hate mosquitoes. Actually, despise and loathe the idea these irritating insects exist. They have constantly forced me to take up war-like defense tactics each time the wretched little tormentors invade my air space. You would probably agree with me if you knew how often I've been stung with jabbing needle teeth. Stinging bites that leave me itching like an old hound dog scratching the mange.

These two-winged diabolical pests have bitten and stung me at least a zillion times over the years no matter where I've lived. They arrive in what appears to be squadrons of thousands, attacking after rains have drenched every space within five miles of my home. Just as annoying, they're barely visible, appear out of nowhere like tiny fighter jets to dive, buzz and sting every human or animal they see.

Their heinous, aggressive behavior gives us reason to despise and fear these wickedly clever pests who invade all year long, except for the freezing months, in every place we lounge, eat, or play. And they're sneaky little devils too, invading homes, picnics, pool parties, sport events, and every outdoor activity they can find. They're nothing but tiny bullies swarming everywhere, hiding in every shrub, tree, flower, and vegetable garden, as well as on every inch of lake, river, and pond shoreline, determined to provoke and sting every living soul on earth.

These dastardly little vermin hide in plain sight, stalking at every window and door ready to pounce. Their irritating buzz is a form of mind torture, especially at dusk or after dark, sending me into a frenzied type movement closely resembling a jerky twist and shout dance as I swipe at their whirling hum.

I'm certain they're one of earth's most hated tormentors with one goal, sting. Using their ever-ready needle thin stinger to pierce the skin of any moving creature to suck out blood, which should put them in the category of vampires, is one of life's most exasperating woes! Worse, they fly as fast as a UFO, then hide or disappear as stealthily as an M1 trained spy!

Seriously, military strategists could learn a trick or two from these black-hearted, irritating demons that are infernally cunning and fast as lightning. I absolutely detest these tiny flying creatures we know as mosquitoes. They create havoc for thousands of people across the world who are forced to defend themselves with cans of repellent, fly swatters and other such armory to kill them off. It is mind boggling to know that not a single person world-wide, or possibly out into the universe, would ever admit to anything other than extreme disgust for them.

This leads me to ask why God would create such annoying scoundrels, the worst troublemakers on the planet, and I'm positive Noah didn't invite them onto the ark. But, being sneaky little devils and living up to their reputation, they obviously snuck on board in the dead of night, multiplying as fast as they could simply to aggravate the daylights out of everything on board for forty days and nights. And then forever and ever after every creature had left the ark.

I don't believe I can ever be forgiving of these devil-made sleuths who have annoyed and injured me for years. Some will tell me not to hate or to swear that mosquitoes deserve to die more than roaches, scorpions, and black widow spiders, but that's how I feel. And rightfully so after I've been stung so many times over the year's I feel I've been emotionally scarred for life.

Trust me, I've tried to think differently, but I simply can't trust these devious minded mosquitoes. However, carrying small cans of mosquito repellent in my purse helps me be ready and armed the instant they appear. I spray my sandal clad feet, bare legs and arms, as well as my house, vehicles, patio, and every space around me.

The second a mosquito comes near me it drops from the air like an F-16 fighter jet shot down. Invariably though someone will ask, "What is that awful smell"? There may not be a rosy, sweet perfumery scent about me, but hey, I'm safe.

Cure For All

Today's mail brought six catalogs, of which I normally throw in the trash but today two caught my eye with their catchy name's so I took time to have a look. Oh, my stars, I had no idea there was such a varied group of ailments and so much stuff to relieve or fix the afflictions of the human body.

Glancing though the catalogs I soon realized I was holding answers for ailments of the aged, the retired population, the aching, tired body, me! I didn't know the body could deteriorate to this extent, but, thank goodness, the products offered promised to alleviate almost everything, and change lives to boot.

I'm not sure how my name ended up on a mailing list to receive these catalogs but it might be the fact I joined a senior organization in hopes of getting a few discounts and have all sorts of programs and travel options available. Anyhow, looking through the catalogs was, to say the least, puzzling and intriguing, but also a little frightening.

The names of these publications, obviously, were meant to get one's attention; "Our Changing Body" and "The Feel Good Store", which could be construed as something entirely different. But the point is they are targeting older folks who have a number of dysfunctions, some embarrassing, some quite scary to contend with as we head into our senior years.

I've known for some time my body wasn't the same as it once was; graying hair, new wrinkles, eyesight not quite as good as it once was, and I'm slower to begin my morning. Stiff joints and an aching back make me feel less motivated to "get out there for a good run". Yes, I've tried the ultimate, new mattress that promises more restful sleep, tried adding a few exercise moves, along with vitamins and herbs that promise less stiffness and a more youthful step.

Thank goodness I can color my hair, and use moisture cream to slow the wrinkles; but its preserving the brain power, maintaining my memory, and having healthier lungs and cholesterol that is a concern. My newly discovered catalogs are promising to help with or heal all of these.

This makes me feel safer knowing when the time comes to correct a disorder I've got access to a copper threaded, heat retaining ankle brace, or I can melt away a plantar wart and corns. A foot soak will rid my body of all sorts of toxins, ear amplifiers are available for better hearing, and I can know immediately if I have enough oxygen in my body by using a pulse oxi-meter.

Also available are brushes of every kind; one will improve the breathing of the scalp, while high tech toothbrushes will keep teeth and gums healthy. There is also one to exfoliate dead skin from the body, (eweeee) and scrub brushes for one's feet and toes. Who gets so dirty a scrub brush is needed for their feet?

I hope I never need these items, but they are readily obtainable. Knee and elbow braces, some with magnets encased in natural cotton fabric, wrist braces with special supports for pain and tissue injuries, and a negative ion necklace to promote good health. Why not use only the necklace and you wouldn't need anything else in the catalog? Humm.

Besides all this, there are dozens of items in the cosmetic line that can fix everything. Whiten teeth, eliminate puffy eyes, wrinkle eraser cream, lash extensions, thinning hair potions, and a cream for dry and sagging skin. Dozens of cover up products for the face can be yours for a price; lotions for every part of the body, and shampoos to help every hair problem.

We can also solve embarrassing problems such as smelly feet, nail fungus, ingrown nails, cracked heels, and athlete's foot with healthful products that reach beyond the imagination. We can also alleviate and cure flaky scalp, joint pain, poor circulation, and digestive upsets; all could be gone forever with these treatments. Say good bye to allergies, snoring, ear ringing, skin tags, and cellulite. I'm serious, the remedies can change our life for a price. All are described in detail and very convincing.

No energy? That can be fixed, cholesterol can be lowered, weight loss can be achieved, sleep disorders vanish, and brain power boosted, restored memory as sharp as an elephant! Healthy hair and skin can be realized again with breakthroughs that will set the medical world on its ear; all right here in these catalogs! There is a vitamin or herb to rebuild every cell in your body, plus, secrets to everything! Healthy heart, blood pressure, and lungs can be restored with vitamins and herbs. Secrets of a healthier life can be ours at last!

Perhaps I should invest in these miracle products, you never know what could go wrong in the bat of an eye.

Although, I may have to do it slowly as I'd not be able to make the house payment if I buy everything to fix what ails me. Well, they do promise to refund your money if you are not completely satisfied. One even stated I'd be profoundly changed without sacrifice and be remarkably happy. I'm not sure I believe that, but hey, when it comes to my health, I need to make sacrifice's, however I don't want to be the healthiest and best looking broke and homeless citizen out there!

The Agony of Summer

Is it my imagination or are there more grouchy people than usual out and about? I could be wrong, or perhaps a little sensitive, but there seems to be a lot of grumpy complainers making themselves heard in nearly every place we step.

I'm not sure what's causing so many to be in such a foul mood, however, there are hints being thrown about it could be the hot weather that's causing people to gripe and moan. I bet that's it; it's likely the weather. Thank goodness that will change soon, but it seems pointless to be such a grouch over the weather; whining, raising a fuss, believing the suffocating, hot temperatures will never end.

Seriously, it's strange how difficult it is to convince some people this shall pass. We have a scorcher of a summer every year, so it shouldn't be a surprise to anyone what the weather is going to be. It's not like it's a sudden surprise every summer, it's not a big mystery for heaven's sake. So, its puzzling why people wouldn't plan ahead as soon as the daffodils died out, anyone who's lived through one of these summers should know the hot humid summer months are barely a day or two away.

Don't complainers realize their ongoing moaning is annoying? Don't they realize their mood could put the rest of us in a cantankerous state if they don't get a grip, come to their senses and quit grumbling so much? Honestly, it's such wasted effort, we're smack in the middle of a sultry hot summer known as the punishing stagnation of dog days. It's hot; it's blistering hot, smothering us hot, and it happens every year at the same time.

Sizzling hot summers are a situation we can't do much about other than stagger through them, spend more time in air-conditioned comfort, calm the steaming season with cold drinks, and become a seeker of cool places to kick back. Plan a vacation or trip to a mountain park, to a seaside beach, or add a fan to your backyard retreat, veg out in a hammock, and just chill.

Unfortunately, those who lack the ability to make plans for the hot summer are always going to complain, be nit-pickers about the heat even if living in a tropic paradise, and stay in a grouchy mood no matter the season. Some will use the hot summer months as an excuse to be twice as crabby as they would normally be, or its possible they want attention, using the heat as another reason to snivel and gripe.

Sometimes I honestly believe when temperatures soar into the high 90s or stay over 100 degrees for days on end these folks turn into even more of a cranky person. They exploit the daily news and use personal upsets to shout out surly comments on how they feel, then state it's the hot weather making them irritable and snarky.

I'm not sure that excuse will appease listeners to their complaining because there doesn't seem to be as many weather grouches when it's bone-chilling cold out. What's the difference? Seriously, ice, sleet, and zero temperatures can make one just as miserable as a hundred-degree day with no air-conditioning.

Although, I have to admit ongoing fussing and daily fault-finding isn't heard as much, during cold or snowy weather. That might be because it doesn't linger like the heat, unless you are in Alaska or the farthest north longitude of Scotland or Greenland. And too, we can see winter weather, snap photographs of wintry sights, build snowmen, go sledding, ice skating, and take part in a host of invigorating outdoor winter sports, so it's possible there are fewer complainers during the chilly months.

Too, during the cold, icy winter months we enjoy a certain peacefulness when a carpet of snow quiets the town and countryside. Even if stormy, icy weather presents us with accidents or inconvenience, we don't grumble on about it for weeks on end, so maybe that's the difference.

The heat can't be photographed, which might be another reason people get testy during hot summer days. They can't see what's causing their misery, so they get cross and gripe at everyone and everything. But this is fact, we can't do a thing about scorching, hot days other than hibernate at work or home in air-conditioned comfort, take off to spend the day at a water park, or head out for an ocean beach, a lake, or mountain retreat.

So, quit complaining, chill out, find a shaved ice or snow cone stand or go to the ice cream store for a banana split, a chocolate covered sundae, or indulge in a triple dip cone of ice cream in different flavors. Perhaps when the weather gets the best of you visit the air-cooled library, check out a couple of books, settle down to read in the cool of home or the library and daydream away the summer.

Think positive, cool it. Imagine you might be akin to a hot-house flower, a rare orchid that thrives in the humid summer. And, consider living life a little slower in summer, take time out to sit back with a good book more often, sip a tall glass of iced tea, or a favorite drink with a kick, and pray for an early winter.

Even if it only hangs around for two weeks in January.

The Turkey Sandwich

There is a lot to be said about that great sustainer, the sandwich. This could be nostalgia speaking when I state that there's a sandwich worthy of worship. You know the one I mean. It's made with left-over turkey meat the day after Thanksgiving and Christmas dinners.

Its taste sings out the holidays, calls up memories of the past, and oozes a love you never stop craving. You can't really explain it, but you eat this marvelous sandwich because it's just plain good, and it never changes. Think about this.

Chilled, moist turkey meat left over from the holiday dinner, piled high on sliced bread, spread with mayonnaise, and topped with lettuce, it's simply perfect. Some might argue it's just an ordinary sandwich, but it isn't. With every bite Thanksgivings past might rush by and who you were with, or where, it's a type of nostalgia that floats through your mind.

Turkey sandwiches are available in practically every restaurant and available every day of the year. Most are made with packaged meat pressed thin, sometimes resembling the plastic package it comes in. In some restaurants they might have fancy names, the Paradise, or Club, or a Turkey BLT, among other catchy names. They all feature turkey, usually lettuce, spinach, sprouts, or other greens added, sometimes bacon, ham, avocado, tomato, onion, cheese, pickles, a spicy or sweet spread, or a flavored mayonnaise or mustard.

It might be served on a choice of breads, wheat, rye, croissant, sourdough, burger bun, or French bread, then a choice of sides are offered to enhance it. Fries, chips, coleslaw, beans, potato salad, and more, so what is the big difference? Well it's hard to explain, while those sandwiches taste great, they just aren't the same as the day after the big meal turkey sandwich. Trust me.

During the years I visited my parents' home for Thanksgiving with my young children enjoying the most incredible meal anyone could ever hope for. Mother would keep back enough turkey to make sandwiches for us to eat on our long journey home. Those sandwiches were filled with love and magic, they were like a tonic that cheered us up when miles from loved ones. They were the taste of home to us, an extension of our holiday during the long trip. And too, soon after the children gobbled up their sandwiches, they fell sound asleep.

When I traveled in far-away lands, I would eat turkey sandwiches often, finding each quite distinct, always delicious and interesting. In Athens, Greece one thoroughly enjoyed was designated as a turkey sandwich, but I'm not sure it was because it had been cooked in such unique spices, spread with an unidentifiable sauce, topped with a white cheese, and tasted so heavenly I don't know if it really was turkey meat. But it left an everlasting memory with me.

Another sandwich enjoyed in France was slathered with spicy mustard and a thin smear of caviar, uniquely tasty but not quite what I'd call a turkey sandwich, I think it was a French version of a turkey or maybe it was duck, which is popular in France. Still, it was scrumptious and different, a real treat. One eaten in Italy proved to be a near out of body experience. Turkey meat sliced tissue thin, obviously cooked in several savory spices, piled high on fresh-made bread, then served with a wine laced tomato-garlic sauce to dip it in. It was like the nectar of the Gods, but then Italian cooks are known for creating delicious secret ingredient, unforgettable dishes. In this case, my near feast of a sandwich gave an enjoyment similar to a near out-of-body experience, but the exotic setting in a small, family Italian café, and the wine, may have helped.

The closest I've come to loving a sandwich as much as the plain-as-day, day after the holiday turkey sandwich was in an old and quaint New Orleans eating establishment. The Cajun aromas that swirled and permeated the room, floated out the door to draw people in like a Revival Preacher. It was a turkey sandwich unique beyond anything I'd ever tasted. The meat had been cooked in a spicy brown sauce, mixed with duck and crab meat, piled onto puffy-just-baked bread so good there aren't words to describe it. I've never eaten anything like it since and probably never will. It's quite possible the festive atmosphere and surroundings, and the spices that rearranged my taste buds would never allow me to forget this heavenly sandwich and the memories if left me with.

The turkey sandwich from that roasted holiday bird is intimately connected to our heart leaving a truly magical taste, a craving, and a memory. Possibly a taste of rapture, a moment where ordinary becomes great and our appreciation and longing for that day after turkey sandwich never leaves us.

If I'm ever elected to an office where I'm in charge of making a law, I'd pass one to give us The National Turkey Sandwich Day. We are entitled to it the day after Thanksgiving and Christmas because it's a joyfulness that can never be rained on, besides we deserve it.

Worries, Woes, and Distractions

Even the sunniest of personalities have worries when stressful uncertainty hovers. However, this meant to calm statement, "Don't worry about it", usually falls on deaf ears. Which is a normal reaction, because humans are natural worriers and have been anxious and distracted over something or other since time began.

Seriously, we worry too much. With dozens of situations arising daily to push us over the edge of coping, we fall into confusion, become concerned, and then begin a fretting and woeful type behavior. To my way of thinking, it's very possible, and scary, to think the worry gene is part of our DNA, passed down from our ancestors, the caveman.

Think about it, cave people worried day and night; how to find food, a warm place to sleep, and were fending off animals wanting to make a meal of them. They then moved on to worrying about surviving floods, rain for forty days and nights, the plague, in-fighting with family, revolutions, wars, earthquakes, now we've nervous about the possibility of nuclear annihilation.

We fret about finding and keeping a job, where to live, and do we have more than ten items or less to go through the express line at the grocery store. We wonder if the moisturizer we're using will help, overreact about cholesterol levels, diet, our weight, and become frantic when it comes time to find a mate.

Once we do find a mate, uneasiness piles up. How can two live as cheaply as one and should we have children; the truth, don't have children, your worries expand ten-fold. On top of that the government adds regulations and taxes to our daily life to the point we're constantly broke, can't afford a vacation, and stress over what is really in our drinking water. See!

To clear up a few troubling thoughts on our food; there is no such thing as the four food groups rule to follow anymore. The new rules have taken over, multiplied, divided, and are nearly impossible to figure out. My take on this is the easiest solution - eat whatever you want!

As we age, concerns dog us if we've saved enough for retirement, should we be using solar energy and electric vehicles to be eco-friendly. How are we to afford a funeral when it comes time because they've become quite pricey, possibly a bit pretentious, a tad overrated.

The thought of a breakdown in our home is ever present; which appliance will fizzle out; refrigerator, washing machine, or the cooking stove? Just as troubling, if we buy a new one, we bite our nails from dread after reading the operating guidelines and warnings!

It's the ongoing changes and hazards lurking in every corner of our home and town that give us reason to be concerned. Clothing stores, grocery stores, and restaurants are all baffling in some way or another, seriously. With a thousand brands and sizes to search through we feel distressed finding clothes to fit, agonize over restaurant menus that have dried food smeared over them, and are troubled wondering why a tuna sandwich with chips or fries, no drink, would cost twenty-five dollars.

Increasing prices at the grocery store drive us batty, preservatives added to everything is downright puzzling, scary, plus will the hand wipes used on the grocery cart really keep us from catching the flu. How do we know if the eggs we buy are from chickens roaming freely, and will pesticides clinging to our fruits and vegetables really cause cancer?

Even our toothbrush harbors germs as dangerous as having a CT machine scanning every living cell of our body. And this old statement isn't true anymore either, "seek and thou shall find". Everything we seek is troubling, making it more difficult to be cheery when we can't find the product we want and scared about what is going to kill us, bankrupt us, or make us sick.

Once upon a time our home was the safest place to be. Today we've learned the comfy mattress we sleep on, the pretty paint on our walls, and the insulation in the attic contains chemicals that will make us sick. Now a new report is telling us there are harmful pollutants lurking in our air, water, and on our lawn!

The once enjoyed cigarette, pipe, and chewing tobacco will alienate our friends and could give us cancer. Just as troubling, too much sun can harm us, but the right amount is good for us, too much alcohol and coffee will impair our mind, but drinking the right amount is good for our heart. See what I mean!

With so many threats to our safety and health, it seems we risk dying while trying to live, eat, and stay healthy. Every day brings possible peril, unnerving events and thoughts spring up to the point we could be labeled the nervous generation. Plus, we're teaching our children to be concerned with such things as playing in or falling down in the dirt, which is full of chemicals, and if they ride a tricycle, a helmet tough enough to blast off into space is required by law.

Transporting children from one place to another can be worrisome, requires strapping and encasing them into a specially built seat with materials used to construct submarines! Plus, it can weigh as much as seventy-five pounds, must pass a long list of government regulations, survive crash tests as trying as a moon landing, and is so pricey it could give adults another reason not to have children.

Threats to our health are shouted out on television, in magazines, and social media to the point where we are anxious and troubled constantly, and not sure we can get through the day without some sort of calamity. Think about it, government researchers and ecologists have ordered our food and medications sealed in near impenetrable plastic material in order to protect us from who knows what.

Our fears and courage are tested non-stop, we struggle to manage our sanity, and appear edgy when facing obstacles demanding trust. Especially dealing with the IRS, FBI, EPA, NRA, SPCA. This should be a warning that any organization that has only capital letters to identify it should be scrutinized.

We are so stressed we need a break, a get-away vacation to a resort by the sea, a theme park to keep us happy and entertained, or a visit to a far-away place we've always wanted to see. But getting there is stressful. Airplane travel can be discouraging with so many regulations we feel like petty criminals, plus the fear of a passenger coughing out germs of a contagious illness is ever present. And, just as important, will I miss my connecting flight?

Going home from merely an hour away can also be worrisome, what calamity has happened while absent from the homeplace? Did the toilet overflow, was the stove burner left on or did a robber invade? Did the cat unroll the toilet tissue again, and did I remember to close the garage door? Maybe Scarlett O'Hara's attitude will help, worry about it later.

But I tell you what, if those "officials" tell us we have nothing to worry about, we are seriously in trouble. Any attempt by them to reassure us we don't have a thing to worry about would for certain have us come down with a permanent case of anxiety. Worse, develop an ongoing case of the heebie-jeebies; doomsday for us because there is no cure for that calamity.

Luggage, A Fashion Statement

The suitcase was a marvelous invention that helped travelers haul possessions across the globe when leaving home for a night or two, or for long periods of time, or far-away places.

This utilitarian case was the very symbol of traveling, embarking upon a voyage of importance, going somewhere of immense necessity, or touring for leisure. The case would hold the most personal of belongings, extra clothing, or important papers, books, tools of a trade, among other items.

While both small and large cases were usually kept locked in case they were dropped, or an attempt to open it was made by someone other than the owner. A traveler's case was very personal, usually held possession to keep close, items of value, jewelry, guns, and other treasures to keep safely locked. When leaving home or the workplace it was best to protect our case from thieves who were known to set about to steal suitcases and travel bags; not much has changed.

Travelers on horseback had their own design of the case, referred to as saddlebags, made of sturdy leather. They could hold personal possessions, medicines, secret items, or any item they wanted to hide and protect, usually a gun. Saddlebags were a horseman's suitcase and always left with him when he left his steed elsewhere.

The impressive suitcase began as a small carryall made of leather, sturdy cloth, sometimes wood, usually with metal corners and hinges, and a lock. Such a case was referred to as a valise, satchel, briefcase, backpack, train case, or garment bag. Larger versions to tote more of one's possessions were called steamer trunks or chests that could be carried aboard ships, trains, or carriages when leaving one place for another for long periods of time.

Today the suitcase or steamer trunk is no more. It's graduated to being referred to as luggage, barely resembling the suitcase or trunk of yesteryear. Luggage is now quite appealing, colorful, unique designs, and sturdy enough to survive a trip into space. Today we find luggage made with a variety of tough materials that appears nearly indestructible, and its characterized as the epitome of a fashionable accessory, a status-identification carry-all.

The look and shape of traveling cases have evolved over the years as time and needs changed. We filled our automobiles with cases, trusted them to airplanes flying across the skies, took them with us when hiking, biking, or riding in various modes of transportation. But it was the French designer, Louis Vuitton who first created fashionable bags in the late 1800s. High-end cases, bags, and trunks that would propel suitcases to become desirable pieces to own and be seen with then and still today.

We aren't exactly sure when the first suitcases were used but there is reference to types of luggage and trunks used during the Crusades to transport equipment and weaponry. We know the word luggage first appeared in the English language when it was mentioned by the Aristocrats as early as the late 1500s. The first suitcase in modern times was invented around the 1870s and evolve to the sleek wheeled cases we see today as we dash through airports. The wheeled case became the most coveted of all travel bags following it's invention in 1972. However, there is evidence of a type of wheeled luggage dating back to 1848.

Now that travel has become affordable to every social class of people, rich, or not, the increase in travelers has turned luggage making into a booming industry, developing into both expensive as well as affordable bags. This means stashing one's belongings in a brown paper sack to travel anywhere is passé, not a hip or fashionable type bag to carry, which wasn't the case a few years back. Paper and various odd types of bags were seen as a common means to carry a few small things, usually when traveling by bus and train.

For those who go visiting overnight or long term anywhere in need of a piece of luggage can head out to a big box store, a department or discount store to find an affordable, semi-designer bag or luggage of any type. They vary in sizes, colors, and prices ranging from twenty-five to around a five-hundred dollars, making any get-away easy, reasonable, and pleasurable.

But for travelers who want to identify themselves as fashion setters, happily schlep off to high-end luggage stores, a Neiman Marcus, or fashionable boutiques the likes of a Louis Vuitton or other couture designer stores. Those with no thought to price will spend hundreds of dollars and upwards of six thousand for a designer bag that will surely make a statement. Apparently, there are travelers with a need to identify themselves as rich and fashionable, purchasing luxury items that give a fashion pinnacle of pleasure that screams out, I'm first class.

Seriously, luggage is in, it's it! It's beyond functional, now cool and the accessory to own and be seen with. If you haven't been in an airport recently, you're missing out on entertainment, a first-hand insight into what everyone seems to have selected as the savvy, stylish accessory one can carry or roll. One would also observe an odd assortment of how people of Earth dress, which if Aliens from a far-away galaxy were among the crowd they would be snapping photos to share with non-believers back home.

I'm not into marching along to popular culture by snagging a $1,000.00 designer bag to zip aboard airplanes or to the must-be-seen-at vacation spots. Just give me a nice, practical piece that's lightweight and easy to maneuver. While it's great to look stylish and relaxed while traveling with a nice piece of luggage rolling with ease, I can't seem to bring myself to give it to an airline employee to throw, possibly shatter, when it lands five feet down to the ground. Nor do I want my nice piece of luggage and its contents to disappear into luggage purgatory, which does exist, trust me, this is a place where luggage disappears never be seen again, much less found.

Rest assured, luggage really does get lost and if you've never lost a piece of luggage, you're lucky, I know, it's sheer hell. Lost luggage is the dirtiest word to the travel industry and can ruin the best of vacations for the traveler who experiences the loss. So, heading out to a big box store, a retail or discount store to find a sturdy, semi-designer case-bag-luggage piece that's affordable in any size or color to make a get-away pleasurable, is smart and seem a practical buying option.

Think about it. Beautiful, stylish accessories are mood altering, even if I found a piece of luggage designed by

Michelangelo or Picasso, I doubt I could bring myself to spend thousands for it, nor would I trust the airlines with it. Besides, who among us wants to risk losing a high-end piece of luggage to suitcase hell, just as bad, stolen. So, practical me, believes sticking with my sturdy, lightweight, roller bag, which was last year's model found on sale at the discount store for half price is the perfect travel accessory.

The List

The trouble with making a list, it's never finished. They get misplaced, lost, or somehow vanish as if a magic wand had been secretly waved over it. In my view, this makes the effort of making a list a waste of time. Still I make them, but it drives me batty to the point I vow to quit.

However, I find I need to make lists, it's a sensible choice, even if it seems a type of crutch to give a false sense of being in control, or perhaps gives the feeling we know what's going on, when we don't. The whole idea of list making gives me doubt I'm doing nothing more than writing down items I need and yet still forgetting half of what I wanted to remember. Even more annoying, half the items on the list are never found!

Lists are repetitive and futile; well, they are, along with the fact they become worthless if left at home when you set off to purchase the items on the list. Or, while in the store you can't find things on the list, again, this means the list is never finished. Quite an annoyance because a list is supposed to help us with a chore, tell us what to do, what to buy or look for, what stops to make, i.e. gas, bank, pharmacy, dry cleaner. Unfortunately, the list doesn't tell us everything because we forget to write it down.

If we can't find everything on the list, we move it to next week's list, which is a bummer, plus the kicker to this. I wasn't always forgetful and disorganized. I never made a list when I was single and motherless; parenthood apparently does this to a person, well, it does sound like a good analogy, I'm serious.

When you're deprived of sleep, as new parents are, one's mind doesn't work as well as it did before. Think about it.

At two in the morning quieting and feeding a crying baby means an abrupt, frightening awakening, usually not getting back to bed until four a.m., worse you can't go back to sleep. If you do fall briefly asleep, you're awakened again at six a.m., but your mind is all muddled and slow. This behavior on a regular basis can lead to forgetfulness, I'm not kidding, it's been documented as happening to parents who suffer sleep deprivation.

As children grow so do lists because there is more to do, hence, a longer list, and more lists. A mother can't write down everything that needs to be done because there is so much, and it constantly changes. Example, wash clothes and blankets, put wet wash in dryer, fold dried clothes, get registration for pre-K finished, pick up toys, dash to pharmacy, pick up the baby's prescription, get gas, call dentist, call plumber, pick up dry cleaning; see what I mean.

Your mind fills up with so much to do and things to put on a list you will invariably forget half of it. By noon, you have several lists started because you began one before preparing dinner last night. But too often challenges cause your mind to drift, especially if the children are fussing, arguing over toys or who touched who. Or, while cooking dinner your toddler vanished in a mil-a-second and began flushing toys down the toilet, of course the toilet overflowed.

By morning, you start another list, get sidetracked and forget to put several necessities on that list. Still, making a list does have its advantages; you most likely will get half the things on it done. But if you don't have a list when you head out to the grocery store your mind will go completely blank once you cross through the doors with a shopping cart. So, one should keep a permanent note attached to the steering wheel that reads; 'Don't forget the GROCERY LIST'.

However, the errand list and household chores list is so long you know you can't finish it, but thank goodness you made a list or you would have forgotten to pick up an anniversary gift for your parents and the dog's medication at the vet. Although, writing things down on paper is now passé, smart shoppers and the younger generation put lists in their phone. This will of course solve the problem of the vanishing paper list.

Still, keeping a running list of everything to be done in the house, every errand outside the home, and a tally of groceries needed, can be time-consuming. The lists have become so long it's impossible to get to the end; this could result in grouchiness or bring on anxious behavior. With so many interruptions, taking time to feed the kids, bathe the kids, take the kids here or there, you become scattered in thought, overwhelmed with lists.

Also, the errand list can be difficult to read because you jot it down in a rush before you forgot what you were thinking of. Example, pt clts ndy, fld, awy. That means put wet clothes in dryer, fold and put away. On the errand list, dp lib instructs you to drop books at library, hadwr ovbub. Translate: go to hardware store for an oven light bulb. See what I mean!

But it's the grocery list that rattles your nerves. As soon as the list is made, put it in a purse or wallet so it's not forgotten.

And for God's sake, and yours, put it in some sort of order so you don't criss-cross the store two or three times.

When a hurried dash out is a must for things that are immediate, things you're out of, need right now, but when you get there the store is out of stock of the item you need most. If shopping at two grocery stores for the sale's you'll never find at least one of the items on sale. The reason, items in one store are not placed in the same layout as the rival store so it takes twice as long to find half the things on a list. So, the smart plan, consider shopping at the same store every week.

The trick to making an errand list work, write down the order of where the store or place is located. In other words, be organized. Don't go to the library across town from the grocery store then backtrack where you began because you forgot to get gas while at that end of town.

Hopefully a day will come when everything on the entire list can be crossed off, even the non-food item list. But crossing things off can be daunting because most of the items and chores on a list won't be found or done. So, no matter what, the list can never be fully finished.

Then you say to heck with list making, but it's addictive, especially when you discover life is not manageable without a list. Example, a birthday card wasn't mailed on time, the car safety sticker wasn't gotten on time either, or the dog's annual shots were forgotten. How could this happen? Bet they weren't on a list.

Accept list making is a must, but crossing off every item on any list will most likely never happen, so just keep moving the unfinished or un-found items from list to list. This becomes the list you will most likely never finish - the house chores. Seriously, it's a documented fact so just deal with it, rather like enduring a conversation with a blowhard braggart.

You know the list I'm talking about, it's the one you've been writing on for months, the one to remind you to fix things, it's the fix-it, get it done list. The odd, broken things you can't bear to throw out, surely, they can be repaired you reason. Or we procrastinate over taking on difficult or boring projects that have been put off for months.

What an easing of mind if the Christmas gift buying list could be finished on a timely basis, the holiday errand list, groceries for the holidays, what a sigh of relief if they could all be finished a week before the big day.

However, those aren't nearly as comforting as believing, or hoping, no one has you on their hit list!

Don't Let the Bedbugs Bite

I'm not sure what's going on with nature right now, but several news reports have put us on alert. However, this information has us questioning why recent news releases about bedbugs have been brought to our attention as if we are facing an invasion from locusts and frogs, worse, Aliens.

How could such a nasty little bug become so important and in the news on a regular basis? Well, it seems this tiny misery of mankind, the bedbug, has multiplied into the bigillions, and invaded nearly every place the human race resides.

It's true, news of their invasion has been featured on the news, in magazines, and written about in major newspapers across the country. Apparently, it's become a serious concern for every social class and business. Owners of upscale, fancy hotels are distraught, nice franchise motels in towns, cities, and on major interstates, along with residents of clean and not so clean homes and apartments across the country are in a panic.

These tiny blood-sucking bugs, around since the ice age, are moving in everywhere, munching on the masses no matter where they reside or sleep. They've taken over homes and businesses, any abode where humans live, driving some to the brink of insanity. The bites from this tiny bug cause endless itching, red splotches, inducing ongoing whining and cussing, often resulting in the bitten losing all signs of common sense.

Bizarre as it sounds, The Associated Press reported homes are being burned to the ground by their owners to rid them of bedbug nests. In one such city, Cincinnati, Ohio, quite a nice place to live, there have been several documented incidents involving these annoying, miniature insects being the cause of homes being set ablaze. How could this be happening?

A local station, WXIX-TV, reported several bizarre cases of burning out bedbugs taking place where cities have experienced ongoing infestation problems. The question of why the infected homeowners are not using the services of pest control when warnings have been issued is beyond comprehension. Seriously, can anyone give me a valid excuse?

After suffering hundreds of bites, with no relief found, occupants of homes, whose mental stability should be questioned, came to the decision that burning out the bedbugs nesting places was a good idea. Didn't the fools realize the nesting place was the bitten occupants' house? Unbelievable. Obviously, this tactic seriously damaged or burned the entire home down. Where the residents were initially injured, confused, and shocked they were left homeless.

What moves people to believe it's practical to douse mattresses, sofas, or any sitting or sleeping area with combustible fluid then set a match to it? Could it be for the insurance, or do the exasperated actually believe their idea of burning will work? The thinking of, "We'll burn those dang critters out" leaves one to believe bedbug bites have a toxin that induces stupidity.

With a trillion advertisements out there for cleaning living areas, and dozens of insect- killing products and pest annihilating companies, why would anyone resort to setting their furnishing on fire to rid the home of bugs? Is it possible after being bitten the bug's venom obliterates the ability to consider, think rationally, or seek alternatives? Either point, something is terribly wrong when residents are driven to the brink of deliberately burning down their homes.

Perhaps infested cities should appoint bug delegations or intervention panels; I mean it's possible to teach people how to safely go about killing off these annoying little pests. At least bring in nature experts or the animal control specialists; they know exactly how to deal with snakes and raccoons invading homes. Most likely they'll be able to eliminate the bedbug population in a snap, at least one would think.

If the officials can't get a department to deal with this surely there is a federal agency that could step in and fix this problem. After all, our government does have a history of dumping a lot of money into studies on what should be and can be done when a crisis is happening.

The government was in charge of the mosquito population explosion that was making people sick, so they developed a poison chemical solution to spray in residential neighborhoods, and cities. Some time back they also set about to clean up our air and oceans so perhaps they can wipe out the bedbug population with newly developed methods they are always dreaming up.

Surely this type of study and research will be taken up by a team of government specialists who will come up with proof that there is a favorable solution to the eradication of bedbugs? At least one that is more successful than burning.

That is, provided the ecology department of our federal government hasn't declared them vital to the ecosystem.

The Laundry

For various reasons, I despise doing the laundry. It's too much work, boring, unsanitary, and a repetitive chore that's never finished, this is fact. I should know because I've been washing dirty clothes for so many year's I don't want to remember the number of years. Naturally, this has made me hate the idea of doing the laundry week after week, year after year, and I'm not alone. Seriously, I don't know anyone who likes or enjoys doing the laundry, nor have I ever heard a single person say, "I've got to spend more time washing clothes, I love it".

Here's proof to back this up. In every living space and home there are piles of clothing, towels, sheets, rugs, and more to be washed every week. After it's washed and dried it's dumped out on beds, the sofa, on top of the dryer, and in the dryer waiting to be put away. After days of ducking around it and watching family members search for a matching pair of socks, yell and scream a favorite shirt they finally found has been shrunk, ruined. Worse, some items turn up stained, torn, missing buttons, colors from another garment faded on it, or just as bad, a few items have been left unfolded for so long a child outgrows the clothes waiting to be folded.

Laundry is stacked in nearly every room to the point the place looks like a laundry service drop off, which, to me is unimaginable how anyone could enjoy doing laundry. At some point one asks if it would be easier to throw away mountains of laundry and simply go out and buy all new stuff. Seriously, why are we keeping shrunken, faded, stained, unraveling shirts and towels, no elastic underwear, at least twenty unmatched socks, and pajamas with tears and stains?

Unfortunately, as most of us know, doing laundry is one of the basic needs of man/woman since forever and ever but seriously, I'm just plain fed up with the whole idea of this ongoing task. Although, as we say, thank goodness for laundry service and dry cleaners. Still, the practice of keeping our household items and clothing clean, neat and folded, hung in a closet, or taken to a laundry service usually falls to the female of the house.

And it's not a surprise this mindset has created uncountable disagreements between male and female, children and parents, each looking at laundry as such a pain in the neck chore, or a task no one wants to take on, a job so disagreeable it's argued over on a weekly basis. Plus, doing the laundry was never mentioned in any wedding vows I've ever heard. Nor was anything ever discussed concerning who would take on the task of fishing out rocks, sand, and crayons from the washer or cleaning out the lint filter or dryer that had melted chewing gum, candy, crayons, and other unidentifiable stuff scattered in it.

I mean what woman wouldn't want something more meaningful in her day than standing over a four-foot pile of dirty clothes tasked with cleaning dried oatmeal, mustard, and ketchup from pajamas, shirts and pants? Or the job of constantly spot cleaning, peanut butter and jelly, mustard or unidentifiable food drippings from children's good church clothes. Or, on a daily occurrence clean baby spit-up formula; throw up, kid poop, snot, and mysterious stains from nearly every piece of clothing, sheet, and pillowcase children came in contact with.

It must have been the cave woman who realized the stink and dirt needed to be washed away at some point from piles of icky coverings the family wore. Regrettably, taking on the task of cleaning such strange smells and unknown stains from garments doomed women from that day forward, to forever being the laundresses.

Thank goodness, this practice by women has evolved for the better with modern washing machines but it's still an unsanitary job, disgusting, downright scuzzy, ongoing work. But for some reason, the job of sorting, spot cleaning, and decision making to wash or throw away hasn't gotten easier. In fact, it's become a type of punishment because the job must be done week after week and the worst of it comes after a family vacation, which can set one's nerves a jitter.

Another thing, well several, there are washing rules to be followed, otherwise unspeakable consequences happen. White clothing items can't be washed with colors, towels and sheets need to be washed separately, and dark clothing isn't mixed and washed with anything. And heaven forbid if a red sock or t-shirt accidentally gets in with white items. The white clothes become permanently pink.

Delicate items, lingerie, sweaters, and wash and wear items have their own cycle and soap. Rugs must be washed on a heavy-duty cycle and placed evenly in the washing machine so they don't get slung off balance during the spin cycle. This really does happen, matter of fact a consequence for not following this rule; the washer will be thrown out of balance and simply stop, usually when full of water. If this happens the rugs will be soaking wet, weigh fifty pounds each, and near impossible to remove from the tub of water! See what I mean.

Of course, one must know how to spot clean stains, choose a laundry soap that doesn't have harsh chemicals to upset the balance of a septic system. Bleach should be carefully measured, more importantly, know how much can be added and when to use it. Fabric softener is a must because if it's not used clothes will wrinkle or turn out stiff and scratchy after drying.

Lord help us if a washer ever breaks down, especially if it's filled with water. Just as bad, the water hose breaks and floods the laundry area, which seems to happen way too often. This of course sends one into shock, followed by a lot of mopping up work, or costly repairs.

If that doesn't scare one consider the dryer woes; this is a whole new group of challenges to deal with. Apart from discovering gum or crayons melted inside the dryer and all over every piece of clothing, finding a half-eaten peanut butter sandwich in a child's jacket pocket has melted peanut butter onto every item in the dryer which makes the dryer forever smell like peanut butter.

This is also a common issue. A child standing in front of the dryer, appearing traumatized, screaming, "my blankie", and will not stop crying until a damp blankie is pulled from the dryer and handed to the child! Or a child's favorite stuffed toy, that was so scuzzy dirty the health department would condemn it, falls apart during the drying cycle. This means you have to hide it from said child until it can be sewed back together.

One horrible experience for a family was when the youngest child gave the cat an unscheduled bath then placed the very wet cat wrapped in a towel in the dryer. The sounds echoing from the dryer brought the entire family to the laundry room. That poor cat never quite seemed right after that. Just as nerve rattling as a pet in the dryer, the dryer catches on fire; this is the most traumatizing experience a mother, laundress, could ever have.

Dryer fires are indescribable, scare us half to death, and leave one scarred for life. For some reason cleaning out a dryer lint filter doesn't register as an essential chore related to laundry rules. So, after years of lint packing in tightly along the length of the dryer hose to the outside vent, the dryer heating coils become overheated and burst into flames. The sight and smell of an entire laundry room and clothes dryer on fire is mind altering; I won't even go into the after-effects this has on the psyche, or cleaning up the mess, much less comments from the fireman.

But these are not the only concerns of doing the laundry. Have you looked at the aisle of products displayed in the supermarket? Oh, my stars. It can leave one dumbstruck trying to choose. There are laundry products made with chemically enhanced ingredients that could clean rust from metal gutters, others are biodegradable, cruelty-free, no animal testing, plant based, with bleach, without bleach, scented with flowers, fruits, herbs, or hypoallergenic. I'm sure manufacturers have planned others for future release to confuse us even more.

My mother washed once a week, she used plain old soap, baking soda, bleach on everything and no fabric softener. She hung our clothes on a clothesline to dry; she brought the laundry in the house and put it all away in the same day. That was it. Now we have computerized washers and dryers that are so complicated the user must go online to study an instruction manual to learn how to operate it!

Me, I think I've reached the point where everything will be taken to the laundry service where they wash, dry, fold, and hang items on hangers. Although, I've given this a lot of thought and its leads me to believe those nudist groups were on to something all this time after all.

Classless and Clueless

This is not one of the most serious problems we need to be worrying about, but it's a concern that seems to be cropping up more often. The worry, what has happened to classy people, their regard for appearance, but more puzzling, what has happened to manners among the masses?

Seriously, there are a lot more people asking as its obvious there has been a downturn in polished courtesy over the past few years. While there are some that possess a hint of care, manners, and tact in dealing with rules, challenges, or guidelines for graciousness, others just simply don't want to be bothered with any effort for courtesy in any form. Their attitude might be to shrug and say, so what, while some feel manners are just a bunch of stupid rules.

This should bring a head jerk of concern for those who don't seem to care how they look or conduct themselves in public, or even what they say. I'm not sure it will, but hopefully there is a possibility they might. Sadly, there aren't many giving thought to where they are and how they appear to those around them, or how their spoken words are perceived. Just as puzzling, some don't seem to know what politeness is or how to behave graciously.

Some don't believe it makes a great deal of difference how they look, speak, or what they have thrown on to appear in public; they're simply trudging through life. My perception, although I could be wrong, there is less pride among people, less concern, and less interaction with any type of happy or polite greetings by the new breed of classless folks whose numbers seem to have increased by a huge percentage.

Personal manners and etiquette once considered an art form in defining character and respectful upbringing has all but disappeared. Many today are completely clueless to what manners are, and what is the proper, respectful presentation of self in any setting in or outside their home.

It never occurred to me that at some point I'd encounter a woman out shopping wearing her pajamas and house slippers as if it were the latest fashion trend. It wouldn't have been quite the shock if she had dashed to the store at six am to pick up a package of coffee, but this was at three o'clock in the afternoon. She was attired as if getting ready for bed, or just getting out of it.

Oddly enough she looked as if she had seriously come to shop. She had an entire grocery cart nearly full of food and soft drinks. It's possible she has difficulty with scheduling time, or perhaps had nothing else to wear that day; it could have been that all her clothes were in the wash and she was picking up soap, and then said, "Oh, what the heck! I'll get a few more things while I'm here".

This event is just one example of lack of thought, or class put into choosing what to wear when going out in public. Sadly, it's being witnessed more and more; even at funerals, baptisms, and weddings, which I have personally observed. This event was eye-opening.

A tipsy-appearing woman showed up at my uncle's funeral wearing a rather short, bright pink sequin dress, very high heels, and a fur wrap. To some that is not an outfit usually chosen for a funeral. I don't believe she gave much thought to what is respectful attire to wear when paying respects to the departed. But it seems just about anything is worn today, anywhere.

She wobbled about half-way down the aisle, sat down on the edge of the pew with a look of a "deer in headlights" sort of blank stare. She stayed barely ten minutes, dabbed her eyes with a tissue, and then left as quickly as she had arrived. Several mourners thought she may have wandered into the wrong event; still why would anyone show up at a church in a sequined evening dress and fur wrap in July! Again, maybe her more sedate appearing clothes were in the wash.

I still have difficulty addressing this nut case without falling into a fit of laughter. At my friend Christina's grave site, a man, naked as he was born, streaked right through the ceremony, mere feet from the casket, screamed out her name and threw a bouquet of flowers at her casket. In a flash, no pun intended, he streaked on through the cemetery as if this was a normal ritual for burying the departed.

Grieving friends and family standing at the graveside, heads bowed, when the scream echoed out; all looked up, saw the streak of flesh fling the bouquet, then dash on. Not one person could identify the streaker. We were in shock, whispering what just happened and why? It left each of us to wonder, some with amusement - did Christina have a secret life, or possibly belong to the local nudist club? See what I mean, who would do that at a funeral, where are respect, manners, class? If she had belonged to the nudist group, what a classless way for them to pay tribute to her!

So how do we manage in a world with dwindling respect, manners, and class? How do we tolerate the jeering, impolite behavior, the obnoxious attire, or address impoliteness? How to overlook those speaking inappropriately or with offensive foul language? My concern, are we doomed to return to the manner-less caveman thinking? I'm concerned that type of behavior might spread across the land like the plague.

It also seems we have trampled the whole idea of apology too, those who say they are sorry after doing or saying something they knew was so wrong or hurtful, usually aren't sorry at all. Regret isn't in their thoughts, they simply don't care, don't feel a need to apologize, or even admit they could have been wrong, spoken without thought, hurting feelings, or made a mistake.

Amazing as it sounds, there are citizens who have finished some type of schooling, graduated from either a good high school, tech school, or college, and have come away from it without a clue how to behave, speak, think or consider others. They are simply wandering thorough life without a thought to those around them, no plan, no concern of the feelings of their fellow man, not an ounce of compassion or respect for much.

But the baffling scenario in such confusing lifestyles, few seem to be interested in trying to make corrections. Few speak out or feel any need to offer direction or teach a few manners among friends, family, or strangers. Think how refreshing it would be to witness the behavior that includes sincerity, a little polish, concern for others, and thoughtfulness, plain old kindness.

I'm sincerely troubled the age of class, etiquette, and manners are eroding away, ask if these virtues will become lost to history, our past. Still, I pray that attitude, kindness, manners, politeness, respect, and self-esteem will find their way back to us so that moral character can be seen as who and what a person is and how they feel about themselves and others.

Argue with me, say I'm wrong, or pity me for praying class and manners, principles and goodness will come roaring back, and once again be in style.

The Ever-Present Enemy

Some have long realized the most rewarding, successful, trying, and disastrous result of oneness is the offspring from a union of two people. Getting married is a blessing, a highlight of one's life. Unfortunately, love-struck people often neglect to look to the future and how their long-range commitment to this merger of two could have an impact on their nerves. This refers to the children that come from a union and the relatives that will be inherited.

When we marry the love of our life not much thought is given to who will become our relatives, nor do we attempt to learn much about them, who and what they are, along with personalities. Neither person who agreed to step into wedded bliss considers explaining the complexities of their relatives or their family history to the other love-struck partner, it simply doesn't seem important. Love will conquer all. Honestly, it doesn't.

This seems to be a significant omission by both parties, but for some reason family history is forgotten about when one falls madly in love. Once two people agree to marry, enter into a legal union, the first discussion should not be where the ceremony will take place but to speak openly about who the family is, no matter how painful.

There will be a few surprises, even denial when it comes to plunging hopelessly into an agreement until death do you part. It's guaranteed disagreements, fighting, fussing, blaming, and at times wishing death or divorce will have us part. Still, lovers cave in, accepting what they agreed to when joined by matrimony and agreeing to things they had no idea they were consenting to. Only later discovering what they got themselves into, who the kinfolks are, and more. All this is rather overwhelming, frightening, or embarrassing.

The other surprising discoveries and complexities that will arise when blessed with newly acquired relatives and children that even God can't explain. Our children will at first delight us, then confuse us and torment us for decades. However, an even more frightening outcome of a union of two is how the offspring evolve. Each parent will gain family trees with DNA, personalities that stand out in a crowd, both good and petrifying, that haven't been acknowledged for eons. The newly acquired family passes on to the offspring a bunch of DNA that cannot be explained away. Relatives may be personalities you would never choose for a friend, much less family you want your children to share a bloodline with or even share a home with.

Also, in this new union the mother of the bride or groom is ever present so get used to it. One or the other, if not both will always be advising, suggesting, nosing into your personal life, and home life. It's as if they have taken on the role of producer of the greatest film to ever hit the big screen. Uncle Joe or Aunt Betty, grandma or grandpa drop in unannounced as if it's the local diner. Cousin Emma or Scott might be stopping by to visit way too often, as joblessness tends to afford one extra free time to roam about freely. Who could have known?

Drunks, criminals, thieves, the always-broke, shiftless, lazy bums, welfare leeches, liberals, and die-hard skeptics of any and everything appear scattered throughout family trees.

Know it all's and perfect egoists, financial wizards, beauty queens, and bible thumpers also make up a big part of families. This bunch of misfits, bozos, and tycoons makes for miserable family reunions, holidays, and family must-attend celebrations and funerals. I'm sure writers who create scripts and soap opera shows have attended many such functions to gain writing material.

According to national reports families punch, stab, shoot, and kill each other on a somewhat regular basis. This should not come as a big surprise or shock as blood is not thicker than water, which also makes us believe that ignorance has evolved into stupidity. Another awakening surprise is that normal, sane members of families have been known to move away from extended family that behaves badly. Some never return for a host of reasons. Who can deal with the overbearing, bossy mother or mother-in-law, the drunken uncle, the ditsy or lazy sister, other problem relatives with issues so daunting it's best to choose to live far away, along with having little interaction ever?

Wedlock is however mostly blissful, often an alliance against the outside world. But the producing of children can have a variety of effects on a parent, usually not spelled out to lovebirds embarking upon wedded rapture and to the new parents who are joyfully happy in the moment. The acquiring of family and children, be it one or several, has a unique set of tolerance methods that affects our nerves for the remainder of our life.

Children do not bring endless joy; they produce sleepless nights, family fusses, costly expenditures, and a maelstrom of problems that never end, even into adulthood. From the moment of their child's birth, a parent's life ceases to be their own, moving them to ask over a period of years, what have I done? These questions usually result in more praying, asking God for help, taking up spirits of the liquid type, existing in a state of dull confusion.

Somehow the union of two souls survives their joyful and taxing entanglements with their children long into the golden years, although they constantly struggle to live as cheaply as one, usually because they had children. This of course, isn't always a successful venture, mainly because children take on the same idea as if owning a boat, which is referred to as a hole in the water into which you pour money.

Of course, you guessed it; the world of holy wedlock often leads to fussing and blaming. But there are good reasons for hanging around, it gives you someone to talk to, eat with, and discuss the woes of the world with. Talking doesn't mean listening, which leads one partner to believe they are simply talking to the wall or themselves, especially since the children arrived and tortured each of you into partial insanity.

No matter, as the years pass you are together, share companionship and the mundane activities older folks engage in. Not to mention attempting the art of avoiding the interruption of family visitors, which means you constantly need to be partners and plotters for escape tactics.

Alternatives to visits from family members, overly bossy adult children, and ill-mannered grandchildren leads both partners to practice maneuvers such as ongoing vacations, visits to old friends, some at retirement centers who offer good times, happy hour, or a free meal. This makes for a viable excuse and incentive to visit often, leaving family visitors to find other activities.

Visits to friends that live in another town or state are always a good excuse to get out, away from obnoxious or lazy, unemployed relatives or adult children - the very same children, who are more annoying now than when they were teenagers. Going anywhere can give an excuse for why it's not possible to babysit the grandchildren while their parents escape.

Whether adult, teen, brat, toddler or baby our children are a joy, the 'know it all' species, who can become the enemy. They can drive us batty, tear our heart, jolt nerves, drain bank accounts, and wreck family cars. Our children, big or small, are blessings that keep us real, drama that alters our brain and readjusts our living, the best and worst of merging generations, and numerous ancestors from the blooming family tree.

This is a frightening realization. And since none of us knows what they will become, they are the consummate mystery. Still, they are the love of our life, the post we lean on, forever there, lovable, bossy, and annoying.

Can't Get There From Here

Getting around can be complicated, annoying, and at times life threatening. If venturing out onto America's streets and highways you may find 900 million cars, 430 million buses, 160 million motorcycles, and uncountable bicycles out there at the same time you have decided to get out and about. All are vying for space to go to and from in various modes of transport, at least half are doing so in a careless, irrational, or frightful manner.

Although, one good point to getting out and about, we can go just about anywhere at any time, enjoy being in exciting, wonderful places, here and there, everywhere for fun and pleasure. The downside, we will most likely be risking our lives nearly every passing moment. I'm not kidding. We want to believe everything will be exactly as we need it to be, considerate drivers, good, exotic restaurants to discover in various places, happy entertainment, and that the weather will behave and be pleasant. But this is often not the case.

Thank goodness we have great technology available to help us travel across town or around the world. It's great, a Godsend, but it's often confusing and irritating. A perfect example of confusing technology is the GPS system used to find our way. It's a blessing for the directionally challenged or when traveling in unfamiliar areas, especially cities. The GPS system can help us manage on roadways, streets, rural areas, and in unfamiliar places. The downside, it isn't always correct, or we deal with distracting, confusing road signs that are usually out of date.

It's no secret that relying on navigation systems can be trying, frustrating at best. Over the past forty years, traveling any distance long or short has gotten to the point where it can be challenging. Traveling anywhere has moved along at a clip faster, more diverse, and so high tech that most struggle to keep up. At times travel is discouraging, leading us to believe it's not as fun as it once was.

Today's changes with going and returning seem to blow with the wind. Getting into an automobile, most with computer driven devices, presents us with changing chaos from the radio to windshield wipers and temperature controls. Relying on a GPS to get us to the exact spot we want, doesn't always work. I'm serious; it isn't the perfect answer to get us from one place to another for it's often wrong.

This may come as a surprise, but the robot telling us to turn left in 500 yards should have given the direction to turn right. Why is that? Well think about it. GPS systems are computers that were set up by humans entering the content, directions, and so on into the system. Unfortunately, humans make mistakes.

This could mean a robot is directing someone to turn left into the lake or onto someone's lawn. Don't shake your head, it happens every day. This has caused many a traveler to become hopelessly lost, drive off an embankment, into someone's fence, or onto a recently closed road under construction. Naturally, this produces a string of colorful words not meant for young ears.

You say, that can't be right, I've never had a problem. But 10% of GPS users have been known to have an accident trying to follow directions. Some arrive at a destination ten miles from the intended stop. Yet, despite our grumbles and exasperation with road travel, we have more complaints traveling by air.

Planes are not the ideal perception of comfort, offer no scenery, and sometimes leave us stuck sitting beside someone we would never allow inside our vehicle or home. If the flight is delayed or canceled, we can become stranded for hours, or we miss a meeting, wedding, or funeral, which of course tests the most easy-going personality.

Airplane travel tends to scare us during stormy weather, rude flight attendants stare us down as if we are a loathsome species. Being seated near a screaming child can completely shatter our nerves but worse, a person sitting next to us who accidentally releases gas ruins our day. A canceled connecting flight might leave us stuck in an airport overnight with no way to get home, yet we tend to argue planes are the fastest way to get to a destination. Despite the noisy, hurry-up atmosphere at terminals we must come and go from, we humans are constantly flying.

Trains are a different comparison altogether. A variety of fascinations has always surrounded trains. Songs have been written about trains, young boys dream of disappearing on them, mysteries and murders have taken place on trains, and commuters swear it's the only way to travel from city to city. However, once on-board, trains offer a type of freedom one will never have on an airplane. They instantly take you away, the feeling an adventure has begun, a pleasure like no other is suddenly with us.

The world looks different through a train window, if traveling around Europe on a train the trip may become a romantic dream or quite the adventure. Viewing either sunshine or rain through a train window brings peacefulness, an almost supernatural quiet to the mind. Unfortunately, there is a downside to train travel, delay! Truth be told, it happens often with the most common being stranded in the middle of nowhere, waiting for a herd of sheep, cattle, or buffalo crossing the tracks, or a derailment that may leave passengers stranded for days.

Once upon a time, traveling by ship was the most exciting adventure of all. Great luxury liners such as the SS France and the RMS Queen Mary were the ultimate in travel to cross the ocean to Asia or Europe back quite some time ago. But today we have luxury cruise ships that take the masses to places never before dreamed to frolic, sightsee, and see wonders. Therein, is a whole different set of good and bad, along with odd events taking place by setting off to sea.

It doesn't matter if we leave home for both familiar and unfamiliar places, embark on a vacation close to home, or take leave to find our way in another country. Abandoning the mundane, traveling anywhere can both ease our mind and test the body. Still, we have the pleasure of enjoying or disliking the difference in new places, seizing the chance to love the diverse and remarkable, and have a grand time.

Thankfully, the world has improved in its modes of travel offered, but it's the marvelously multifarious that entices us. We can take in the splendor and smell of the challenging, charming, captivating, outlandish, and foreign places, or feel free to ignore or embrace the hurried or laid-back modes of travel.

This leaves me with this; travel is a joy, scary, unpredictable, yet we seize the chance to take it up, know we're bound to wind up somewhere we do or don't want to be. Or, maybe we'll be impressed with the fact we're away somewhere different and will return with memories that last a lifetime.

A Cast of Socks

Walking around in bare feet is one of the most relaxing feelings we can indulge in, it brings on a different disposition, downright comfort that simply feels good, and frees our feet. Bare feet is a seriously pleasurable experience, rather like partaking in a vice that isn't altogether sinful.

However, if the weather isn't good, cold or rainy, we're thankful for socks, especially if it's bone-chillingly cold and there's a need to trudge out into frigid wintry weather. Our feet love the feel of warm, soft socks before we slip on shoes or boots. But have you ever wondered how something so luxurious and toasty that we depend on has so many names?

Or, have you wondered why they were called stockings many years ago and today we refer to them as socks? We still have the Christmas stocking, but then we have socks with names that are a bit misleading, some sound so confusing that Alien beings from another planet may not understand what we're talking about, and why all the fuss they might ask.

Who came up with the name tube sock, or sweat socks, why hose and hosiery? They all go on our feet so why so many different kinds? Ankle socks, referred to as anklets, were the socks most of us wore as children. Bobby socks were the rage for teenagers in the 1950s and pantyhose seemed a blessing and a torturous punishment to women.

Sheer socks for women were introduced, so they could have a dressier hose/stocking to wear under slacks. Men donned crew socks when participating in athletics, then everyone began wearing them with their athletic/tennis shoes, and have been wearing dress socks in office's, churches and various other venues. See what I mean.

Mismatched socks, stretched out socks, socks with holes, and socks whose elastic has given way can be a real nuisance, but we hesitate to toss them out, why is that? Men often buy two or four pairs of socks that are exactly alike, so no mistake is made resulting in one black sock and one navy color, especially if the lighting isn't good or one is in a rushed state.

As a young girl I heard the name windsock and was confused. My dad had taken me to a small airport where he met with a pilot who often flew him to job sites. When the odd type of flag being beaten about in a fierce wind was pointed out, he commented no one would be flying for a while if relying on the windsock. I was left wondering about such a name, why was windsock used to describe a type of flag and I asked; "Why would someone need to wear a special sock to fly an airplane?"

A popular fun saying in the 1970's was "sock it to me" and children, and misguided adults, often threatened to sock each other in the nose. Just as confusing, an electrical outlet is sometimes referred to as a socket. Some years back people were heard saying they were socking away money for a rainy day, just as odd, the Pacific Ocean is home to a fish named sockeye. See how confusing this might be to children or someone learning to speak English.

This past decade funky socks were the rage. With wild colors, designs ranging from holiday to animals, cartoon characters, planets, stars, you name it, socks were everywhere featuring any and everything that could make a statement about the wearer of the socks. They were splashed with colors beyond imagination or special interest. As most fashions that come and go these funky socks did go; lost their razzle-dazzle, now considered voiceless, passé.

Most of the world loves socks but the funky socks went out with the tide. I'm sure those folks who live in tropic or sun scorched areas, shook their head in amazement. Although, I would think walking on hot sand at the beach or in the desert would burn one's feet if they didn't have some sort of foot covering.

All things considered we have certainly come a long way with socks for they have a history that goes back to the cave man who wrapped his feet in animal skin. I'm willing to bet this is where the term stinky feet originated. Then women discovered they could knit wool from sheep and have comfortable warm woolly socks they could wash. Not long after, they made different colors, sizes, and lengths and socks became a must.

Modern man/woman wear socks of such variety and colors one can own a kaleidoscope wardrobe of socks. Silk, cashmere, wool, nylon, polyester, cotton, among a few of the fabrics, plus a selection of lengths. We have been told our feet are the beginning of one's soul. So, it makes sense to believe our soul can be soothed with a covering on our feet that feels good, especially if the weather is rainy or cold.

For some, socks are a must; think how many armies have depended on socks to keep their feet dry and warm or from getting blisters from the long treks they marched. We put booties on the tiny feet of newborns for warmth and comfort and put socks on our dog's feet if going for a walk on frozen or blistering hot walkways.

We also love our bedroom slippers which are another version of the sock, sometimes worn around the home in place of socks. The slipper is a relaxing covering to slip into, once socks and shoes have been removed, especially after arriving home from a long day at work. Our feet can have a rest, often while we sit comfortably reading, or enjoying a few sips of our favorite spirits soothed by a soft comforting sock or slipper.

The prospect of warm, comfortable, feet covered in a fine fabric is a delicious prospect. However, once the socks are removed and feet dipped into a warm bath to soak, a most healing and therapeutic method to ease our tired feet is beyond soul soothing.

Once there, the sounds of 'ahh' will be heard from a sock discarder.

Practical Safety Tips

From the looks of things most of us are pretty lax about safety practices, be it around the house, out and about, or driving. As a homeowner, or even a living person, we need to wake up to factual statistics telling us we're injuring ourselves to the tune of 40,850,000 accidents a year.

That's right, those are the numbers showing up at emergency rooms all over the country. Thankfully, some of us are careful, but many others are behaving stupidly, carelessly, and thousands are downright clumsy, the rest simply aren't paying attention to much of anything. It's really quite alarming to learn that so many are not qualified to manage the simplest of tools, they don't pay attention to directions, or most are merely not thinking rationally.

Frightening as this is, there is a whole group who just don't care if they, their house, or possessions are safe and secure. This often results in their either tripping and falling from lack of paying attention, or running into things with lawn mowers, boats, automobiles, and a number of other modes of moving about. It's mind boggling.

If one watches the news, goes to the internet, reads a magazine, or the front page of a newspaper you'll see frightening statistics. Accidents, clumsiness, stupid behavior along with crime taking place among the masses is ongoing, non-stop on a daily basis. This should be a clue that we aren't paying attention to what is going on around us.

Being aware that accidents and crime can happen in every space we step into is essential, and should set alarm bells off to entire communities, but it doesn't. Some never seem to grasp that threats have reached all sectors to the point living anywhere has us surrounded by danger. But where does one begin to make their living space safe if funds are short because staying safe is a costly venture? Seriously, if you try to buy a gun, install a state-of-the-art electronic burglar alarm, get an attack dog, or try to stay healthy, one needs money to take up any method of protection.

However, it's a good idea to look at all options for safety because an ordinary or sophisticated computerized alarm system for your home might have you shelling out hundreds of dollars. But then, surrounding your house in inexpensive barbed wire isn't a good idea, plus it's downright tacky looking. So, spend a few dollars on something reasonable and suitable because it's certainly worth it. Although, the downside to an alarm system is learning to use the confounded thing! And, once you learn how to use it, it's a given you or someone in the family, or the dog, will accidentally set it off on a regular basis.

A gun might be something you want to own for both protection and hunting, either way both are a bit pricey. Plus, you'll be required to have several types of background checks and tests, unless you are a criminal. It takes big bucks to purchase a gun, again, unless you are a criminal, when one can be gotten free because criminals steal guns, among other things.

While dogs are man's best and greatest protectors, again you need to spend money; seriously, it's worth every dollar though. After buying a dog it will need training to become proficient in guarding your home and possessions. During this time a ton of money will be paid out to the trainer so your newly loving canine protector can be effective and guard your possessions and home properly. Of course, it can be costly feeding a dog and paying ongoing vet fees, but again, it's worth every dollar because your dog becomes your best friend and family member.

If you want a dog the size of a dust mop that yaps as if a serial killer is at the door when it's only a leaf falling to the ground, those adorable little fuzz balls are rather expensive. FYI, a small, cute dog will cost just as much as a hunk of muscle kind of big dog. So, go for the bigger dog as the friend and protector and then indulge in that lovable small dog as the fierce barker.

Although, if a large threatening type is purchased prepare to have a messy house, chewed up shoes and sofa pillows, lots of poops in the yard, and spend more on food because fifty-pound bags of food have to be hauled home every week. A note of preparedness; a good-sized guard dog will eat as much as your 6 foot, 300-pound Uncle George. But your dog will become a loyal and loving member of the family, again, worth every dollar.

Leaving the television on or having a timer turning lights on and off in and around your home while you are away just doesn't do it. Neither will asking a neighbor to come around checking on the house or mow the lawn, put the trash out for collection, or park their car in your drive because, one, burglars are on to that plan, and two, no one has a neighbor like that anymore.

Some people resort to putting up a sign that states, "Beware of Dog" when they don't really have a dog. This too is not a good plan because burglars usually break in anywhere, the downside if you do have a dog; the criminal often takes along a steak, so they can distract your big dog.

A weapon in the form of a gun requires you go through training, get a license for carrying your gun, and has you alert 24 hours a day as if on caffeine injections. A gun gives one a good sense of security provided you know how to shoot, so you spend money for shooting lessons. If you don't have good training or are past the age of sixty-five your reaction time may slow down to where the gun is useless, or you accidentally shoot yourself in the foot.

Staying safe in your home might require staying away from ladders and electrical tools. Ladders are especially dangerous to those who have reached their golden years. So, to enjoy the pursuit of happiness and no broken bones, consider hiring a handy-man service to do anything requiring a ladder and everything around the house and yard requiring tools with an electrical cord. Again, this can be a costly expense, but money shouldn't take priority over your safety.

Think about this too, you do not want to be referred to as Clumsy Carl by the staff of your local hospital emergency room, or hear this on a regular basis from a spouse or doctor, "What were you thinking"? And for heaven's sake don't even think about working on or replacing anything that requires an electrician or plumber, unless you are one.

There aren't any accurate statistics to point out here but I'm willing to bet 95% of those who tried using a chain saw without first reading the warning instructions that came with the device most likely wound up at the emergency room after this statement. "Geeze, how hard could this be?"

It's equally disturbing to learn that some of us aren't good at certain projects. We tend to bungle chores, trip over things left out of place, or fall off step stools while changing a light bulb. This of course tends to leave one perplexed, feeling downright stupid, clumsy, or bruised when attempting chores that result in an accident. Also, keep in mind it might be a good idea to forget about taking on any repair involving a roof, garage door, or tree trimming at your home, let someone else take the fall so you don't have to respond with the statement, "Things didn't go as planned".

To annoy us more the government constantly scares us to death with a bi-zillion warning labels, restrictions on practically everything we eat, use, or want to take part in. Doctors counsel us constantly to do or not do this or that; our own television scares us silly with warnings of ongoing diseases and every failure known to man and God that could happen to our body.

And for yours and your family's sake try to stay up to date on changing highway rules, drive with care, don't worry about drivers honking you, you're driving the speed limit. Plan trips out carefully; take up an offer to have a family member or friend drive on occasion.

Stay happy, don't mope about, it's depressing, and we all know depression can shorten our life, so live in the now happily, no matter what is going on around you. Don't listen to the overwrought weather scientists either, they will try to convince us we'll all be swept away by floods and hurricanes at any moment, worse an asteroid could hit Earth and destroy us just as it did the dinosaurs.

Just as annoying, so-called researchers are yelling at us for trashing the planet, pointing fingers saying we're destined to rot and ruin, the Earth is melting, and the sea and its fish are disappearing. Overly nervous psychiatrists are into the doom and gloom too, offering statistics that sound frightening. Alcoholism is a growing problem, stating we should look at the possibility of cutting back on the wine, beer, and spirits intake in an effort to limit dependence. While this sounds serious coming from a doctor, it may be just a tad over the top coming from those who are supposed to make us feel good about life.

An observation to consider, naysayers seem to always be there to take the joy out of the happiest of times. Imagine trying to convince us we're doomed and that living a full, exciting life, dancing and eating might shorten our life, and celebrating it with spirits could be risky.

So, I say, get a dog if you don't have one, that way you will always feel safe, have a companion, and feel loved. Or add a cat to your life, cats are nurturing, calming, and independent with a knack for kicking back and enjoying life. Good news, some people think cats don't care or understand, but they do and can teach us how to ignore woes that mean nothing after four or five hours. They are also great teachers on relaxing and napping lessons we didn't know are so relevant to our psyche.

And seriously, hire a handy-man fixer upper so there is more time to enjoy relaxing with that refreshing drink, cold sweet tea, wine, or spirits; or that special cup of hot tea the

British swear can solve every issue that might plague us. Pay attention, according to the experts you never can tell if today will be your last day here.

Talking, the Art of Communication

As a species we have come a long way. We evolved beyond grunting and pointing when mankind first discovered we could get something across to another by pointing and making sounds. Talk has changed the planet.

It took a bit of time, but we eventually progressed to where everyone was speaking coherently, had something to vocalize, and began conversing with anyone who would listen. Which in my opinion has reached beyond revealing just how smart or unaware an individual is.

Today we're faced with a world of talkers, the downside, they are in our face constantly, and unfortunately, some never seem to shut up. Especially those TV news reporters and talk radio hosts. Seriously, the human race has had so much to say over the centuries that they came up with several hundred languages and zillions of methods of getting the word out; it's overwhelming to try to fathom the immensity of it all.

Dictionaries were created, books and long documents were written, plays, speeches and more, progressing to talk radio, talk shows, meetings, and conferences to talk, talk, talk. Speaking with a variety of phrases, announcements, and pledges became the norm and we as a people evolved into a bunch of non-stop talkers, gossipers, loudmouthed chatterboxes.

Aliens from other plants have come to watch and listen for even they can't quite grasp what all the non-stop babbling is about. They, I'm sure, think of us as windbags, yellers, and confused expressionists. While we made attempts to communicate with each other over the centuries, created words to convey our thoughts, acted out in displays by arguing, ranting, or muttering, we became obsessive talking professionals and poor listeners, now the Aliens more than likely want us to just shut up.

Over the years, we moved on to torment each other with frightening sales pitches, dreadful jokes, shouting, and book-length tirades, as well as gossip, so much useless information that it feels as if a landslide of dirt has hit us. There is so much mundane and utterly boring talking that some seek solace in places of quiet, giving the impression talkers are neurotic and shy people are loners, dull, or snooty.

It has been said by those who have studied ramblers, orators, and heart-to-heart talkers that there has been an awful lot said unnecessarily by these motormouth fools. Their constant gabbing and opinions tend to vanish in the wind and the listener gets the impression that non-stop talkers tend to speak a lot of nonsense, gossip, tell lies, embellish the situation, or are simply repeating hearsay.

Over time, it appears we have wrung out every word until it's simply dried out, which is a type of suffering like a dull headache that some feel is a form of torture. Words that seem to cling forever during speeches, prayers, lectures, and more, the paragraphs flow into each other as if the speaker is reading five or more chapters of the King James Bible.

When music and entertainment were created, it was magical, however it has evolved to the point it's become blaring sounds that people can't even grasp, much less hear because it is so obnoxiously booming loud. This has led people to begin talking over the noise making it impossible to hear each other, so people begin talking louder, yelling, and fuming because they still can't be heard.

The masses continue talking for fun but that too is beginning to fade. People have become angry believing no one is listening, so they seek out in other ways to grab attention by talking about their anger, grievances, and opinions, generally annoying listeners. Some have taken to brainstorming at conferences and gatherings, demanding they be heard as they criticize any and everything that displeases them. Overall, the outbursts are viewed much like a boring nut case with the complainer in need of better communicating skills, or they are just plain spitting mad believing the world has held them up as human sacrifice.

Still, disgruntled groups and whiners continually discuss changing everything going on in the world, reforms that would give them reason to feel in charge, important, for they feel they've finally been heard, or hopeful they will be heard. This practice has since become somewhat competitive for the disenchanted. They can now feel brilliant, listened to, when they often aren't.

Defense of opinions, greenhorns with complaints, and the disenchanted wanting to be heard would be shouting out their quirky thoughts to their own kind - a group of bellyachers and whiners who seldom get much right or make any sense. But no matter, as long as the feeling of what was being said was believed important by the talker, they were semi-satisfied. Still the speaker, or speakers, seldom if ever believe they could be wrong, offensive, or boring, had too much to drink, or just simply don't quite have it together. They have something to say and by-god it's going to get said.

Foul words that were once taboo began to creep into everyday conversations a few years back, delighting and entertaining some, offending others; no matter, these words had to be spoken. Cussing could be fun, became competitive, flung around with excitement over the fact we had a roiling sea of nasty and hateful words we'd mastered. They were happy to speak them loudly, often, inserting them into everyday conversations, which gave a feeling of freedom.

Recreational talking, communicating sensibly, and rational thoughts with words were tossed aside as new means of expression became an art. We wanted to entertain, be noticed, explain how we felt, saw or did things in our own way. Never thinking the rest of the listeners considered them a blow-hard, obnoxious bores, confessing personal woes, or on a tirade of disrespect, the speakers believed they were entertaining.

Keep in mind it is fun when we hear lighthearted, sing-song conversation. Listen to stories of glee, where the best restaurant can be enjoyed, happy vacation trips, funny stories on events or family gatherings and celebrations. To hear arguing, gossip, mean-spirited words, or ongoing complaining only shows up the uncivilized and disgusting among us, not the pleasant or intellectual character preferred.

However, everyone needs to be listened to, but could it be toned down a tad, lighten up on the griping, the irritating or foul words spoken? Step back, try to find the positive and the good, the best and worthwhile, explore speaking of happier subjects and times, and take on a more responsible, optimistic, and enjoyable attitude toward communicating. Face the fact that miserable and unpleasant talking should not be dumped out publicly.

Consider the fact of speaking hate, disgraceful sentences, and offensive words give us reason to conclude that the talker is a shouter of nothing of importance or worth, hailing from the town of Lamebrainville.

Need a Lift?

I'm sorry to bring this up but women need to know valuable facts affecting their personal life. I mean this isn't gossip or a bunch of hooey, its documented reality. When you realize this is a reoccurring annoyance for women who, for decades, regularly experience the inability to find a good fitting bra, you'll better understand.

Shopping for a bra is frustrating, affects our mood and often turns into a rather pricey purchase. It's a daunting challenge, irritating, and can shake one's confidence in their shopping ability, plus it takes so much time you just want to scream.

Men have no idea what women go through when it comes to shopping for a bra. Nor can they comprehend how disappointing the job is. Listen to this; finding the right fit in a bra is close to impossible because boob sizes, body shape, and weight are different for everyone, so the whole ordeal of finding a good fit in a bra is basically nothing more than potluck. The other depressing aspect of this, the bra barely lasts twenty washings.

Looking back, I don't remember this issue getting the best of me when I was younger. I never gave bra shopping a thought, simply bought the prettiest lacy one in the size that seemed to fit and wore it with nearly everything. I bought a strapless bra to wear with an off the shoulder evening dress. That was it.

Regrettably, the whole world of undergarments changes practically overnight for most women. The search for a better fitting bra to give a lift becomes an ongoing hunt beginning shortly after the first child is born. It's true, boobs change as soon as women have a baby.

Not long after experiencing the joyful occasion of motherhood most moms notice a need for a lift to their boobs, something found to be quite unsettling. Facing the fact a bit of extra help might be needed to hold up their slightly sagging boobs is quite deflating. Most likely coming on gradually, change we didn't immediately notice to our once perky boobs.

This has come to be a seriously and often discussed subject among woman; right up there with the subjects of men, sex, make-up, and losing weight. Anyhow, I'm sorry to say this; sorry because this situation is genuinely overwhelming when we realize our boobs have given way to gravity.

Our bodies change with time, which means the search for a perfect fit bra continues. The truth, change happens, which is so annoying and costly as the hunt for that pretty, lacy, seamless bra, one that won't ride up, or lose it bolster-ability in its promise to give our girls a bit of lift goes on.

Seriously, blame the fashion magazines for giving us false hope, leading us astray by featuring slender models with perfect figures wearing flawless-looking, well-fitting bras. They are showcased in sexy, pretty, matching bras and panties, strapless bras that look great, along with dozens of choices in colors. In reality, few to none fit us like one's pictured on models.

Women are also bombarded with all sorts of choices, spandex, cotton, natural appearing, barely there, push up, support bras, and more. There was once a focus on wearing an 18-hour comfort bra, promoted by a very busty movie legend, resulting in millions in sales. I simply didn't understand for who in their right mind would want to wear a bra for 18 hours?!

While the pretty lacy and feminine bras feel and look good, they don't quite hold our boobs up where they should be. This has of course, challenged a zillion women to buy and try every brand and style to come on the market. The famous push up bra, designed to give us more shape and lift, the sexy, barely-there bras, and those that rubbed our skin red or felt as tough as leather challenged us. The wonder bra that promised miracles, restore our breasts to a more youthful look, didn't quite pan out either.

Anyhow, finding the right bra isn't a new worry, in fact it's been in the forefront of shopping woes for women since 1913. Thank goodness one vain woman went on a rampage, wanting to replace her confining corset with something softer, prettier, and a bit sexy to wear, so she set out to make her own brassiere.

Her efforts to find a comfortable bra sparked a movement and search that is ongoing today. Woman across the world have joined the search trying every design and style for decades, but for some reason, we're still not good at it. Who knew the effort to hoist various sizes of slightly sagging and imperfect breasts would continue for so many years?

Still, we search because heaven forbid, we appear to look like someone who no longer cares. The thought this quest might be unattainable hasn't fazed us, even when great sums of money are spent as we suffer through dozens of ill-fitting bras. However, the pretty ones were enjoyed while those that were too tight in one area and loose in another, the ones that lost their elastic too soon, or were scratchy and uncomfortable, were tossed, still we hoped.

Today we accept our hunts as little more than needed upkeep. Expectations we'll find that magical, great fitting bra to transform our body. One to give us a youthful and feminine, as well as an uplifting look, and correct the droop and give us that natural look we crave.

And then it happened. It was in a department store where images coming from a television set in the lingerie area caught the attention of shoppers. It was a video spouting words closely resembling the gospel of all miracles for the newest discovery in brassieres.

Women of various ages and sizes were modeling computer-generated bras to uplift every size and shape breasts to create the perfect, natural look, support, and comfort. The world of bras had changed. Computer-made bras would never bind, ride up, or show the nipple of the breast through any type of clothing. Shoppers were captivated.

The end to every woman's search for the most desirable, uplifting, comfortable, sexy, body-shaping bra appeared to be finally here. A bra to bring back the perky, youthful look women needed. The fitting specialist, who I thought was a saleswoman, claimed would transform anyone seeking help would be liberated. I was mesmerized.

Sadly, for me a computer made to order bra to improve one area of my figure, which has needs of improvement in various areas I won't go into here, has come too late for me. Nor do I feel isn't worth discussing. I simply couldn't bring myself to purchase the miracle bra that could temporarily transform my outwardly appearance and hold my breasts above my elbows!

Spending nearly the same amount I shell out each month for my electric bill to buy a bra didn't seem to be a sensible purchase this late in life. So, without sounding too melodramatic here is the moral of this saga. Enjoy, flaunt, and cherish your assets during your youthful years, resign yourself to this probability, as time passes bodies of every size will lose the battle of gravity, everything is guaranteed to sag, droop, and slide.

The Choice

Being at home, or where we call home, a place we hang our hat as the saying goes, promises us a sanctuary of comfort, rest, and entertainment. Barring any unplanned commotion that might plague us, such as a leaking roof or something breaking down, most feel a need for a haven of their own despite its quirks and failures.

Our space, abode, or castle is where we feel safe, nurtured. To some, coming home or staying at home brings us a sense of belonging, relief, what we love, where our heart is, our explanation of nurturing, satisfaction. Knowing we are surrounded with loving family, pets, friends, things, memories, are what we consider our treasures.

Others may feel it is a stopover place, somewhere to sleep, a hideaway, a prison or possibly a confining type of environment. They choose to make it a location to light at whenever, or it's the residence to return to when no place else is available, while some consider it nothing more than shelter.

To the masses, it's the satisfaction of their own space when returning after a day, or extended time, away, the place where they're at home even if they're alone. Home is the refuge, a private safe harbor away from the outside world, a haven we joyfully slip into that comforts and soothes our mind and heart. A cool retreat, a warm, cozy place by the fire, or our corner of the world where a nourishing meal is enjoyed, it's our familiar place, home to the calm, or the excitement we choose.

We fling ourselves happily into a recliner or favorite rest spot when a long day has made us weary, kick back and do what we wish, which can be nothing, it's heart resting. Those who need the idea of constant activity, coming and going, shopping, frolicking about or tending to the animals or crops may find it difficult to take a break, sit a spell, or relax, but they love home.

Some restless souls crave openness, out and about gatherings, perhaps feel a tad lonely or claustrophobic if they are confined. So, staying busy, exploring, puttering in the yard planting, trimming, in a garage fixing and oiling, or out rounding up the cattle; just plain out and about coming and going is a common everyday activity, it's needed for certain personalities.

Constant activity, more work, meeting and sharing with friends, family, or strangers for fun times, or eating somewhere besides our kitchen is an ongoing necessity for the constantly busy. They find it difficult to spend idle time sorting, organizing, and reveling in the delight of loafing, putting together a puzzle, or simply taking on the art of quiet inactivity in one place.

There is a restlessness to those who may be not be suited to idleness, sitting for hours at a computer or staring at the television for entertainment. Nor do they imagine being idle for any length of time or confined by a task or situation in any way. They might choke from boredom, and so we have the restless, the busy, the must go and do who can't or don't want to disconnect from hobnobbing or possible mischief. There isn't a desire to connect with the reality of quiet, or soothing moments.

When idleness is forced, such as illness or a predicament we have no control over, inactivity can be agitating. Canceled plans become dispiriting and annoying to the busy personality. They reject taking a mind rest, a chance to listen to nature sounds, sit quietly, or disconnect from the party and social scene.

Doing nothing isn't delightful to a busy mind. Taking in a rest isn't doing what the normally busy need, love, or long for. A few hours of cozy calm, time to reflect, time out for quiet with a loved one, time to paint, read, go fishing without guilt, plant a garden, or write that promised novel, can nurture the soul, but for a busy body it's agonizing, self-induced cruelty.

It's a known fact waking up with nothing to do and mulling over what to do with the rest of the day or week can be comforting to some. The freeing up of a day or week brings the unexpected quiet, sensual thoughts and pleasures, the settling revival of a soul, possibly an adventure that allows us to discover unsung pleasures.

Unearthing the difference between plans and daydreams might catch us doing a bit of creative thinking; or taking on an enjoyable and different task never thought possible, it could be life enhancing. Throwing caution to the wind and fleeing the familiar and busy, signing up for an archeology dig or taking that long-ago postponed honeymoon, all undoubtedly bring glee.

If you look around it might be surprising how life can pass by so quickly. Seeking solitude isn't always the best choice, especially if you want to be reminded how good life is.

So perhaps we should pay attention when the world has proven solitude has a poor reputation.

When confined out of necessity or purposely, make life and living busy and fulfilling in ways never tried before. Look at living as the king of holidays, march to a different band just to see the difference because after all, life really is just an endurance test.

"Nothing great was ever achieved without enthusiasm."

– Ralph Waldo Emerson

Heaven Help Us

Why is it when we feel at our wit's end we ask Heaven to help us? When we feel there is nowhere to turn, we're out of options; we look up, and simply blurt out, "Heaven help me!" What does it mean when we appear to beg to the heavens, to God, an Angel, or to an unknown someone or place and we're not sure exactly what is there to ask for help, to give us a hand with something troubling? Are we seeking assistance from the invisible to solve whatever it is we feel is real that makes us feel so exasperated that we need to ask the unknown for extra help?

Do we believe that who, or what, is in Heaven could do much in a crisis on Earth unless we are pleading for God's grace? If that's the case, I don't think we should be shouting. Wouldn't praying be a better solution than just shouting out to open space?

Apparently, my mother thought she could get relief of some sort because I heard her call out quite often, "Heaven Help Me!" I'm not sure her pleading and shouting accomplished much, or that she got any help, still, it seems mothers do this a lot. I'm not sure what, or who, she thought was in the place she kept shouting at. Yet, there is a lot of speculation from all sorts of people here on Earth about what or who is there in that open space because a lot of people keep shouting out asking for help.

I admit I'm curious and need to ask this; has anyone been to the place where they shout out and then returned? Rather, like the Astronauts who went to the moon, then came back to tell us what they experienced. If you heard someone say they had been in Heaven, and now they're back to tell about it, wouldn't you want to see some proof, credentials, or maybe, question their sanity? Especially if they said, "Yeah, I've been there, and this is how it is." Could we even think about believing them?

It's possible some would question if perhaps the claimant was a con-artist or worked for a TV show featuring church services with preaching, begging, and promising by a religious fellow or gal. Remember that woman named Tammy Faye Baker? She was always crying and looking for a new angle or gullible sinner, asking them to send money so their prayers could be answered. I didn't know God asked for a fee for answered prayers.

If I asked these same questions from people who are speculating about Heaven, or those who studied religion, I bet they won't have answers as to why people are always shouting for Heaven to help them. Still, I'd like to hear what they have to say, and I'm sure other people would too, I mean, I couldn't be the only one curious about this.

Honestly, I think people are just guessing about what or who is there to lend a hand, unless its God they're referring to. Another question I have, if we get to Heaven, is there a long line at the Pearly Gates? You know, the gates we are told are there. And by the way, how do we know the gates are made of pearls? If there is a line where everyone checks in, do we sign a contract, something like "Rules to Follow"? I'm sure it would be worded a little like a Homeowners Association Contract; after all, you are going to be there for a while, plan to consider it home.

I believe these are legitimate questions, at least things to know if we go to Heaven. Don't you? This is important too. If we get there, do we have to be nice to those people we didn't really like when we were on Earth? You know the ones I mean. Those who gossiped, made unkind remarks constantly, tormented us, or those who drove us nuts at work.

What about the relative that was just downright mean, and those snooty people who treated us like we were beneath them? Are we supposed to forgive them and pretend their teasing and abusive, taunting language and threats didn't hurt?

Now that we are on the subject of being in Heaven, there are a few things that concern me. I'm not keen on music playing non-stop, I'm asking because I don't want to listen to it constantly. Seriously, can you imagine, listening to mournful country songs or elevator music day in and day out, and God forbid, what kids call music today! I don't relish listening to angels singing all the time either, I mean I like hymns and gospel music, I just don't want to listen to it non-stop.

If I get to Heaven, I would like a little peace and quiet once in a while, wouldn't you? And what do we wear if we are in Heaven? I mean, wouldn't you get sick of wearing white all the time if it's the only color choice there is? At least they could offer something different on weekends, maybe blue to match the sky.

If one is in Heaven, are they awake and happy full time, constantly listening to people shouting from Earth? Is there constant singing? I'm not keen on that because I have a terrible singing voice. I'm sure I'd irritate those who sang well if I were out of tune all the time. Another question, are there assigned

109

jobs or tasks to take care of so everyone feels useful? I'm not keen on being on constant alert if I were assigned to answer the call when someone shouted out, "Heaven, help me".

And what about some of the rules, are you allowed to get annoyed in Heaven? Is "Thou shall not get annoyed" in the fine print of a contract? What if you didn't get enough sleep and you woke up grouchy, is a grouchy mood ever allowed? What about those heavenly lights, are they on all the time? If not, what do you do after dark? Personally, I'm afraid of the dark so I really would like to know about the lighting.

So, the big question is, why do so many look up at the skies and shout, Heaven Help Me? Seriously, is there someone or something to help when you shout out if things get so bad you resort to shouting out for help to the heavens and expect help. If this is the case, why not chuck it all on Earth and take a chance, just go to Heaven earlier than originally planned. At least you would have help close at hand if you needed it, and it is reported to be a lovely, serene place.

I've heard a lot about Heaven, love the idea it's there, and certainly hope I'll go there. Surely, I won't go to Hell as I've tried to live right. Besides, I've heard all the bad and terrible people are in Hell so it's not a place to even consider visiting, much less staying in especially if there are a bunch of meanies there.

Perhaps each of us should curtail asking for Heaven's help and just sort out our problems before we get there. Seriously, from all the talk, it's the most relaxing, trouble free, heavenly place to be, which means we can leave all our troubles behind.

CLASSICS

The following short stories represent several of Carol's classic, fun essays, and popular reads previously published in several venues.

She outlines annoying, unsettling goings-on in a world that leads us to believe it may be spinning out of control. Her insights and wisdom on working woes, the uproar over meat, fur, and cheating gives us new meaning to progress.

According to Carol, being disorganized or incompetent isn't all bad, odd behavior is common, and taking up napping is enjoyed round the world by those who need a kick-back rest, so indulge yourself she advises.

She promotes traveling but warns us to be on alert, cautious if we take to America's streets, roadways, and interstate highways. She praises lard, agonizes over cowboy boots, waiting, and getting a little help, asking why we lose so much, and speaks frankly about our absentmindedness.

She gives us a rundown on why we should stay close to friends but be wary of family, offers her take on good food, especially avocados, and urges us to enjoy life no matter who is complaining.

Her laugh out loud view on the reality of living life, our failures, lying, glitter, and truth-telling gives us reason to smile, agree, and disagree.

Think I'll Drive Next Time

I've had it with flying, and I'll bet you have too! Seriously, I'm through with airlines. After booking a flight, paying extra to fly on a guaranteed day and having purchased a prime seat, I would arrive at my destination in four hours. An hour before boarding, the flight was canceled! The delayed, rescheduled flight with a lousy seat had me changing planes, finally getting to my home city seven hours later.

How can the airlines do this and keep any respect? I don't think they expect it anymore and one can certainly see why. Not only is it impossible for a person to expect to arrive on a timely basis, getting comfortable traveling on an airplane is next to impossible, actually it's not even an option anymore. Just as disappointing, fear of an unsafe flight is no longer at the top of a traveler's worry list!

Seriously, a trip to the airport for a flight is only the beginning of what will be a challenging trip, most likely have you dodging rush hour traffic, taking detours around highway construction, and facing dare-devil drivers racing to get somewhere in record time. These obstacles are just a start of the surprises awaiting today's air traveler choosing to go from one place to another. I'm not kidding.

The task of finding a parking place at an airport can be rather trying, finding the right shuttle bus to the terminal, unloading the luggage, and locating the check in area all certainly contribute to fraying nerves. After walking what seems a mile to check in, you hand over suitcases full of

112

irreplaceable items to a robotic appearing airline employee, who questions the contents as if you are smuggling contraband. Your luggage, holding your carefully chosen, neatly packed clothing and possessions, is then thrown into the black hole of luggage gymnastics hell. This of course raises the question - will my luggage ever be seen again? These thoughts linger the entire trip, contributing even more to your tattered nerves.

Boarding a commercial airliner today stretches one's patience to the point a normally mellow person might become grumpy or distressed; and in some situation's has them teetering on the edge of breaking into tears. Next is security purgatory, which throws one into spasms of confusion. How can a photo ID be so scrutinized by a uniformed officer, whose sole purpose is determining your mental health, then stares you down with such disdain you ask, "Why am I flying"?

The biggest annoyance is yet to come, the security search; how did we get to this point! Being treated like a criminal, under suspicion of the worse dastardly deeds, asked to shed several clothing items in the presence of at least fifty strangers, your body personally searched and x-rayed for apprehension of who knows what is confusing and degrading! It's enough to cause a passenger to crack from stress and embarrassment.

Once on board your carry-on bag is stuffed in an over-head bin or squished under the ten- inch by four-inch area under the seat in front of you. Finally, the chance to sit down where a surprising awareness is suddenly realized; the fastest way to turn a nice person into a grumpy one is the seat. Not only is the seat hard and lumpy, it is so narrow you are squeezed unmercifully, making sitting quite uncomfortable, plus there is little to no leg room. Seriously, the seat is so hard it's a form of torture guaranteed to require a chiropractor's help the next day.

How did it happen that flying can make us depressed and grouchy, hold us in such suspicion, and cram us into a shrinking seat space that normal-sized, much less tall or overweight people, can't fit into? And the minuscule space set aside for a toilet might easily hold a broom, but it certainly doesn't allow a person weighing over 125 pounds to fit comfortably, much less sit!

This is just as unnerving. When did eating and drinking on an airplane get so pricey? A beverage and a two-ounce bag of snacks will cost as much as a prime steak! A free meal, the size of a frozen dinner, which isn't very good, can be had with a first-class ticket purchase. But it's served by a jet-lagged, unsmiling flight attendant, and for good reason, he or she had to endure the same security scrutiny as the passengers before boarding the plane, then face a bunch of grumpy, pushy, tired, and stressed passengers. None of whom can get comfortable in their cramped seat.

With a miserably uncomfortable seat, concern for one's luggage being lost and never found, and will the plane land in time to make a connecting flight, has deplaning passengers' turning into nervous wrecks. Some resort to chugging stiff alcoholic drinks in an effort to cope, others look wide-eyed and in painful shock. Add concern for what germs have been spread by sneezing, coughing, flu laden passengers, and the feeling of doom might consume us.

According to the American Customer Satisfaction Survey, thirty-five percent of airline passengers are unhappy and dissatisfied to the point they hate flying; I'm one of them.

Think I'll drive next time!

Glitterphobia

This makes me feel rather odd; but mostly it annoys me. I don't like glitter, period. Nor will I touch anything glittery under any circumstances. I want nothing to pass through my hands or into my home that has sparkly glitter on it. Truth is; I'd like to slap some sense into whoever invented it because I hate the stuff with a passion.

Seriously, I avoid anything with glitter; greeting cards, gift bags, holiday decorations, especially craft stores where practically everything is glitterized! But the worst thing about glitter; it's created a phobia! Yes, a phobia, which I find quite peculiar. Unfortunately, I have it.

Don't laugh. Hundreds have it; most sufferers are male, which makes me somewhat of a stand-out. Anyway, it's a real phobia you can find under mental health on the internet with a medical description name of Sparkalaphobia! I didn't make this up!

It's possible my phobia began with a greeting card when glitter came off onto my hands. I touched my face, where glitter stuck, then migrated to my eyes, and within hours I was in the emergency room being treated for a scratched cornea! It cost me hundreds of dollars. That's when my conflict with glitter came to be.

Admitting to my friends I have a new phobia has been a little difficult, actually somewhat embarrassing, almost painful. Well, I do have a few aversions to several things, but I don't let on that I do until I'm actually in a situation where it becomes obvious. The number thirteen has created a bit of distrust for me, and a black cat crossing my path makes me hesitate because I do wonder, but I'm not alone in this. I also suffer with being claustrophobic when it comes to elevators, tunnels, and closed-in places, this naturally has created a few troublesome moments I've been forced to explain.

The point is, when I first brought the subject up about my fear and hate for glitter, I was at lunch with friends, only silence prevailed. Bursts of laughter followed, then, an interesting discussion took place questioning how such a phobia could exist. Shortly after that we discovered it really was a documented phobia.

Usually, when my friends and I are together for our lunch gatherings we only complain about our looks or clothes, console each other, lie a little and make light of bothersome things, then discuss sales and hairdressers among other things. Friends and family do that for each other. This situation got a tad bit loud and controversial but eventually my friends ended up consoling me for having to deal with such a fear.

Think about this, all that glitters is not gold; it's a type of ground up glass and plastic, which can linger in your house and car for years. It attaches itself to everything you wear, anyplace you sit or lie down, requiring you carry one of those lint-roller-thingies everywhere you go for fear of glitter.

My children and friends have sworn they will never give me a card or gift that has glitter attached to it. Unfortunately, my daughter responded with, "Get a grip mom, that's not normal." When told one's behavior isn't ordinary, it tends to

117

be unsettling, but I can't help myself, glitter is simply an awful ordeal for me.

Confessing I have sparkalaphobia concerns me a little. However, a friend assured me it was okay, she should know since she sees a therapist to deal with her fear of spiders, arachnophobia. I needn't fret she said, everyone has something they hate, fear, and can't bear in any form. This certainly makes me feel better to have someone in the know validate my phobia as okay without having to spend a ton of money having a therapist question me about it.

Her therapist indicated most phobias come on subtly over a course of time. Dealing with an ongoing, in your face annoyance or fear, interfering with your way of life to cause discomfort or anxiety, is normal. Well, yes, dealing with spiders in her house, spinning webs, leaving piles of crunched up bugs in every corner freaks her out. Unfortunately, this phobia keeps her on edge, but she is a better housekeeper, checking for and cleaning out spider webs in every corner of her house, nearly every day, which sounds like a clean freak phobia to me.

On the other hand, there are some things that are simply uncontrollable, and the belief that you can deal with them is a relief, but the reality is, I'm not sure. Anyway, I might as well go public with the fact I absolutely hate glitter, have a fear of a few things that don't come up too often, but they are still there and now my secrets are out there.

Going public is good my friends say, it will most likely keep me from ever seeing glitter again. The best part is that it may help me deal with my ongoing annoyance with glitter because now the chances are slim-to-none I'll ever have a speck of glitter anywhere near me.

Forget About It

I've talked about this so many times it's becoming rather troubling to think what the outcome of my forgetfulness might come to. And I'm worried if I keep having these blank blips of forgetful-ness I might have to consider seeking help in some form so to better remember where I left certain things, where I've put my keys, and what is that woman's name.

But here's the situation, it's never been a secret I've been forgetful on occasion for years, parenthood can sometimes have that effect on the sharpest of minds; don't laugh, its documented fact. Although, while there are things, events, and people, I wish I could retrieve the memory of, there are others I'm quite happy I've forgotten.

I've met thousands of people over the years from work, social events, church, and life. Unfortunately, I remember very little or nothing about much of anything we ever discussed. I'm serious, some events attended were boring, uneventful, dinner conversations were sometimes hum-drum and small talk was at times stale, so, party memories have all but slipped away.

I should remember conversations had with famous people I socialized with years ago, a few friends were famous, and we had grand times together many years ago, but as time passed, we lost contact. Conversations, laughter, secrets, all lost to time. My husband asked how is it possible to not remember a thing said with so-and-so. Art events, embassy dinners, awards, and more, poof, they're gone; I remember great times happened, but I moved on.

I can recall a few important aspects of the past, some only vaguely, but it doesn't bother me that I can't remember what impact they had on my life. This could be a good thing most have gone from memory, especially if they were embarrassing. See, forgetting isn't all that bad.

Still, there have been times I've wished I could remember a few people, events, and happy times from the past, but I'm doing well just to hold onto what is in the present. Forgetting is most likely best referred to as senior absentmindedness, which is something I hate admitting. Although, I suppose it's fairly common as my friends have complained about being forgetful too.

Of course, there are those who possess a good memory, but the fact is as we age and step into the golden years, it's just another thing we have to deal with. There are medications, herbs, vitamins, and such that we can use to improve our memory, which is good too. However, I'm not sure I should be spending half my life savings on pricey self-improvement techniques praying they might actually work and help me remember a little more. What I'd really like is something that helps me remember only the necessary things, not the annoying or embarrassing stuff.

One bright opinion came from a clinical therapist who treats people with personal issues, such as phobias, addictions, and more, telling us forgetting is natural and helpful. Most people don't mind being a little forgetful, especially leaving certain situations, odd people, or embarrassing times in the past. Embrace the fact that some stuff and people are gone from your memory for good reasons.

There is also a study that proves forgetting can be liberating, especially if it's relatives we aren't fond of, or birthdays, anniversaries, and such. Think of the money we might save, no more loans to family, gifts, or footing half the bill for a family reunion you know you won't enjoy.

What a relief it could be too if we could forget the people we once dated and party friends we hung out with years ago, now we wonder why in the world we hung out with people like that. It would be mind-freeing if we could forget the embarrassing antics of our youth, the clunkers and ugly cars we drove, and the stupid-looking clothes we bought because they were a season fad. Thankfully, I've forgotten the grief my teen-aged children caused, and a few of the relatives I didn't want to spend time with have passed to the Great Beyond so it not a concern.

And I'm happy I've forgotten some of the personal mistakes made, some made with the stock market, investments, or houses bought, all worth forgetting about, unfortunately some we won't. We should feel joy and be thankful we've forgotten about an awful job, annoying bosses, and odd co-workers, even neighbors we didn't like, had nothing in common with, or those who were such sloppy neighbors they drove us batty.

Most of us have suffered in decorating skills during our youthful years too, especially choices like orange carpet, bean bag chairs, velvet paintings and posters for our walls. And, those awful avocado colored and harvest gold appliances. Talk about mentally challenged choices.

I've personally enjoyed meeting interesting people over the years, some famous, several politicians, entertainers, a few met during exciting travels and places lived, for some reason I remember very little about them. The weirdest thing, I have no idea what we talked about, yet some were friends for years. This should make me feel sad, at least reflective, but seriously, what do I know, perhaps none of us really want to remember details of what was or might have been.

Perhaps we should believe memories and facts from long ago may have gotten twisted, altered with forgetfulness, or the people involved were just downright boring. So, it's possible they weren't interesting enough to remember anyhow.

It's these annoying things of right now that I keep forgetting. Maybe it's because I'm constantly dashing here and there with too many things on the to-do list? I sometimes have a list of must call people, return library books, schedule that dental or doctor appointment so I can keep up, stay in the present.

Memory failure in little spurts is a known symptom of older years, absentmindedness happens when we go through life, get busy, work, spread our time in all directions. This behavior may cause things to be easily forgotten or thought of as not the most important. I console myself over forgetfulness believing I've reached an age my mind is full, so it slowly empties to make room for new stuff.

When forgetfulness stalks, consider looking at remembering things by assuming there is not much going on worth remembering for very long. Whatever the case, just move on to something else, get over it. Let it go, whatever it is, forget about it, believe a forgetful mind isn't an imperfect one. And too, perhaps if it was worth remembering we'll keep it, if not forgetting a few things here and there is just fine. It's possible forgetting some things keeps us sane.

Although, someone did say these wise words, I just can't remember who it is and exactly how they were phrased, but it seemed something like this and sounded good. "Remembering makes life pleasurable, forgetting makes it possible."

The Great Flush

Some of life's greatest pleasures are small and lie readily within reach. They can be ho-hum or pure joy. But everyone will agree, some privately, that an effortless push of a handle to flush a toilet might fluctuate between bland and good when put in a category of pleasures.

Okay, why in the world is the subject of flushing a toilet being brought up, and who cares? Or for that matter how can flushing a toilet be compared to small pleasures? Truthfully, this is an educational offering for those like me, a homeowner faced with worry over a plumbing problem, an issue with the government, and the amount of water allowed to use to flush a toilet.

Again, who cares? Honestly, not many give a hoot until the situation stares you in the face. Here are the facts. Home toilets don't last forever, they leak, wear out, and become plumbing disasters, moving one, no pun intended, to set about the chore of purchasing a new one.

As we know, toilet speak is not something people usually get together to discuss. However, we should all know this, an indoor, flushing toilet is something significantly important to every household and business. If you don't believe me, try living a few days with a non-working one.

The modern toilet is one of mankind's most used, and probably taken for granted devices in the world! Seriously, my home toilet was circa 1970s and sounded like water rushing over a hundred-foot water fall when flushed. It constantly dripped, made odd sounding noises, plus it required five gallons of water to enact a flush, then took forever to stop running, even jiggling the handle no longer solved the problem.

Well, by today's standards, and laws, this is wasting water and committing a crime, I'm not kidding. My out of date toilet is an illegal device. It's true. This was news to me because I had not purchased a toilet in eons, nor did I realize there was a law enacted while I wasn't paying attention that required my using not an ounce more than 1.6 gallons of water to flush.

The illegal toilet I had to replace was old, worn out, and worked only sporadically, which is not a device you want to work part-time. The plumber's words of advice regarding the porcelain throne; there is no fix for this, a new one will have to be purchased and installed to meet the government requirement for a toilet. Yep, the government has a law in force that requires every home to have a low-flow toilet when replacing an old one.

I had no idea what would face me when I set out to shop for a toilet. If buying one hasn't been on your to-do list for the last 10 years, you are in for a surprise and will become quite perplexed with the experience. Not only did the government requirement throw me for a loop, I didn't know toilets came in as many various styles as refrigerators. There were approximately twenty different types of toilets to choose from, and yes, the toilet law is enforced.

To be environmentally correct and law-abiding, we are required to install low-flow toilets with an efficient flushing system to save our water resources. That right, our rights have been flushed! We now must buy and install toilets that hold only 1.6 gallons of water!

However, the most bewildering task was to find a suitable toilet. There is the standard low-flow, a high-performance low-flow, or a gravity assisted or a siphon-action flushing type. Choose the wider flapper valve for better flushing or stay with the regular two-inch valve for regular flushing. Select the sleek skirted trap way design, a round or elongated style with a purist look, or opt for a single or dual flush plain one.

We can choose our toilet in porcelain white or cream, or various colors for a price, one with modern subtle curves and clean lines, or with sleek symmetry. There is also a choice for a push button flusher or a left or right handle flusher. Then a decision is to be made on the type of seat; a quiet close seat, a plain regular seat, or add a lighted seat option. See what I mean!

Oh, Lord I pray, please protect our bathrooms from the government toilet police, those ecology nuts, and Congress humans from enacting any more rules for our commodes, the john, the throne, or as the British refer to it, the loo. Whatever you call it, at least pray the environmentalists are finally satisfied.

The Pleasure of Napping

As a twenty-four-hour, breakneck speed society, we aren't getting enough sleep. Seriously, take a look around you. TV and magazine ads constantly remind us we need more sleep, medication of various kind promising deeper, restful, sleep. But the offerings of various type of mattress to solve our insomnia is staggering.

However, the search to find the right one's is frustrating enough to keep us awake at night. Seriously, look at ads offering mattress choices; there are at least a thousand! How can anyone come to a decision on the right mattress by laying on it in a store for a mere fifteen minutes with several people staring at you, including an eager salesperson? As tired as we are, anything would feel restful, perfect. But then the styles and extras involved in buying a mattress are overwhelming.

There are mattress styles offering astronaut-approved foam, several using pumped-in air, pillow top layers, comfort springs, and several that adjust automatically to a person's weight. Even more confusing are the various styles with electrical devices inside to adjust for lying flat, semi-sitting, and who knows what else; the decision-making for that alone becomes overwhelming.

I can see why we become desperate in a mattress store, but the sleep aid aisle in the drug store is beyond confusing. Look at the tired, sleep deprived work force in offices, stores, grocery stores, those guarding our security, moms and dads; everyone is yawning, nodding off, or dead-dog tired. On buses, the subway, behind the wheel of trucks and cars; all of us are half asleep, longing for a restful snooze.

Most of us just want to get to bed before midnight or are trying to get another five minutes after the alarm sounds. We want a comfortable bed and quiet, maybe the sounds of waves lapping at a shoreline, the distant sound of a train whistle, or a soft rain lulling us to sleep. But what we need is a nap. That's right, a daytime nap to rest our mind.

The reviving nap lasting twenty minutes to an hour has been known across the ages as a rebirth for the most tired of souls. A nap gives us a lift we crave in the middle of the day, a boost that has been idolized for centuries.

According to nappers around the globe, napping is one of man's most coveted pleasures, thought of as a luxurious treat, a sensual surrender to free up our body and mind. So why not? It would certainly eliminate trips through the sleep aid aisle and if the body is tired enough, almost any mattress will be comfortable.

So, why not listen to the famous nappers, the Europeans. They nap every day. At noon, just after lunch, they take a nap! All of Europe shuts down, closes up for an afternoon rest. They close stores, restaurants, offices, and stop the presses to take a nap. They awake refreshed, ready to work, more productive and happier. Yet we Americans scoff, drag our feet, believe we might be looked upon as lazy or shiftless if we nap. It's pitiful, insanity for us to purposely deprive ourselves of rest, relaxation, and a healthier, happier existence by skipping the joy of a nap.

Sleep experts, there is such a job, an actual school hands out a degree after one completes sleep study courses. I'm not kidding, look it up, most likely you'll find your local sleep center not far away. Anyhow, those experts have determined, through proven studies, that over half of the human race needs a nap. We're irritable, sickly, less productive, and grouchy, this was actually in one of their reports.

Listen up grouchy people. You need a short snooze, a deep sleep of swirling currents of surrender, a rested mind. A time to revive yourself by taking a few minutes to rest mind and body. The long winter nap is famous, covered with a cozy blanket, sink down into a comfy couch or recliner, have a good book in hand, perhaps a fire in the fireplace and just drift off, shoo all the cares and worries of the week out of your mind and simply luxuriate in a quiet nap.

How about a rainy-day nap? A restful, peaceful drift away rest, awaken feeling nurtured on a drab and cool, gray day. Nothing brings you back to life and makes the day worthwhile more than a nap on a rainy afternoon. It's a 'curl up and forget about everything' nap: work, chores, the coming holiday or visiting relatives, it's the ultimate soothing rest.

The famous catnap everyone should indulge in several times a week is one of the best. Named so for the cat who knows how to slumber away in a sunny window or on a cool patio stretched out in peaceful repose. Cats nap just about anywhere; we should too. Nod off at your desk with your head down, drift off for twenty minutes and wake refreshed, brighter, able to work the rest of the day more productively, a lighter mood around you, a spring in your step.

And the hammock nap? Nothing is more famous than this snooze, laying in the shade, suspended in air, peaceful beyond description, luxurious, restful, a sensuous feeling of being asleep on a tropical isle. It's a first-rate mood lifter, the feeling of complete relaxation with birds singing and chirping in the background, its peaceful and liberating.

And the beach nap, ahh, that's as good as it gets, dozing in the sun or shade, the salty air filling your nostrils is like chocolate; you can't get enough of it. In all truthfulness, many a beach vacationer indulging in daily snoozes at the seaside has been convinced to retire there, or move to the beach permanently, can you blame them! Drifting off to the sound of waves against the shore, dreaming you're in paradise is like no other mind rest on earth.

A nap after Thanksgiving dinner is the most anticipated nap ever, it's a must that gives both the soul and the stomach a rest, frees the mind and makes you feel useful after snoozing barely twenty-minutes. You feel ready to get back to nature, play a game of touch football or chop a cord of wood! It's the crowning rest spell of the season, one to indulge in every day.

Military personnel are famous for napping anywhere, no matter the weather; a few winks will revive even the most hardened of drill sergeants or warriors. Another well-known warrior, nap-taker was Winston Churchill, known for taking a nap every day. He was one of the most productive, decision makers of modern times, a true soldier of the free world. In his memoir he listed napping as one of his favorite past times. He died a peaceful man at age ninety-one, even after a lifetime of tipping the brandy bottle and smoking cigars every day. See, proof a nap is good for the body, mind, and soul.

131

I'm ready to sink into a recliner, head for the beach or a backyard hammock for some heavenly napping; how about you?

Praise the Lard

I come from a family of cooks, bakers, and eaters of good food. When I say good, I mean wonderful home cooked meals, recipes handed down through the family for generations. Recipes with happy memories, stories from salt of the earth people who created some of the richest dishes ever stirred in a bowl or pot. Food to nourish and bring us together, prepared day after day, for holidays, celebrations, funerals, and for the love of family and community.

Garden vegetables grown from the land, nurtured, turned into meals that sustained, remembered in the fondest of thoughts. Meats from the woods, pheasant, turkey, and deer; pigs and beef that were home raised. Chickens from the land, live alarm clocks, roaming freely, produced eggs for family and neighbors, roasted and fried, baked and barbecued with simple spices, soups that sustained were nothing more than pure magic cooked into eatable memories.

Meals for everyday nourishment and enjoyment, baked, roasted, fried, stewed, creamed, buttered, barbecued, all prepared and cooked, most from memory, with dabs, dashes, and pinches of this and that to season. Rich in gravies, onions, peppers, and garlic, vegetables pickled and canned, meats roasted and fried. Baked bread, cake, pies, cookies, cobblers, and sweet concoctions made with butter, vanilla, nuts, cloves, cinnamon, chocolate, and powdered sugar. All made with love and by knowing how much to add, how to layer, or stir just right. Nearly all were prepared with lard, a secret, magical ingredient.

Some dishes might have spirits or cola added, one my grandmother adjusted calling for a famous name whiskey to be added to the cake batter, instead got a substitute of a few dashes of moonshine. It was moist from added lard, sweet and fluffy with cups of sugar and just the right amount of stirring, topped with frosting made with heaps of butter. It was the most anticipated dessert specially prepared for Easter, Thanksgiving and Christmas dinners. I've personally never tasted anything like it no matter what I've tried.

So, you see, food was similar to religion in my family. Lard and butter were used daily in or on nearly every dish of food that was set on the table. Biscuits couldn't be made without lard and homemade bread was not eaten without butter.

Seriously, my family showed no discipline when it came to gastronomic desires because butter was on the table for every meal and lard was stirred in cornbread, biscuits, yeast breads, and in every pie crust. Butter or lard was added to every vegetable, lard was added to every pot of beans, green, black, pinto, red, or navy that simmered on the stove for hours.

There was no shame in my family method of cooking, and the taste of every dish prepared could beat any meal a top celebrity chef might prepare on television cooking shows. A hunk of butter or lard went into every mashed or sweet potato dish, stirred into every vegetable dish, beans, corn, squash, peas, greens. Every piece of chicken or fish was fried or baked with lard, along with many cuts of meat, including dove, pheasant, or deer.

In our home lard was king. When I was a child my grandmother made (rendered) lard when a hog was butchered, when it was used up a metal gallon can could be bought at the grocery store. She made her own butter too, but when it became readily available after the war, she also purchased butter.

My mother smeared a dab of lard, and sometimes butter, on my sunburned nose and on any burn gotten from accidentally touching an iron skillet straight from the oven. A can of lard was on a shelf next to the stove which mother used for cooking and baking. A container of lard was still sitting on that shelf when she passed away at age 88.

In my travels far from home as a young woman I learned lard was used by cooks everywhere. East coast cooks fry a long list of seafood dishes into perfect delicacies using lard, Cajun gumbo and their stewed, roasted, baked anything could not be made without lard. A memory for me to last a lifetime came from food I enjoyed in faraway Scotland. I indulged in some of the best stews and soups to ever slide across my taste buds, and the pheasant dish I was treated to was roasted with spices and a big slab of bacon full of white fat. The story behind that recipe was as enjoyable as eating that unique dish, leaving me to believe it could calm any misery that might ever befall a soul.

Today, I buy lard twice a year because it's used mostly for making piecrust and biscuits. I can't tell my friends I've put lard in several dishes of food I've served to them because they are of the belief that lard means morbid obesity or early death. What a shame they fell for the propaganda spilled out by foodies over the years.

Unfortunately, there are people who believe lives will be spared if they never eat anything cooked in lard. They don't know any better because we have been told for years to avoid it. Blame the FDA (who is often wrong) for convincing an entire nation that lard was bad for us and should be tossed from the American diet. The naysayers, those diet technicians and food researchers, once declared lard to be as deadly as breathing asbestos.

Now we learn lard is praised as being a healthy way to cook, in fact, it's a misunderstood fat because it contains less saturated fat than most of those bottled cooking oils we have been pressed to use. They, I suppose the food experts, whoever they are, have been trying to convince us that bottled oil is healthier. I simply can't believe that, nor do I believe a good cook anywhere south of the Mason-Dixon line would fall for it either.

Think about this, the magic stuff called lard is a blessing, seriously, can you imagine tamales, pinto bean, hushpuppies, catfish, chicken, or those unbelievable Cajun or Cuban dishes not cooked with lard! If you have never eaten pie crust made with lard you have missed one of the world's greatest taste treats.

I'm not a gourmet cook or professional taster, but I do know what taste beyond good, what is bewitching delicious, what food made in heaven might taste like. Nor do I have enough words in me to tell you how good lard makes everything taste that is cooked in it, I can only tell you it's a reason to live.

So yes, pay tribute to the lard each time you use it, it puts the love in our food and revives our taste buds; so, enjoy and praise it. Truth be told, this bit of advice leads me to believe; cooking without lard makes for a lousy cook.

Refrigerator Agony

Have you looked into buying a refrigerator lately? I have, its nerve altering. The cost and process of such a task is absolutely unbelievable. Not only am I having difficulty believing what was spent on this modern-day necessity, but the choices to be made were overwhelming.

The entire process of purchasing a refrigerator has left me dumbfounded. Seriously, the refrigerator I just purchased cost more than I paid for my first car! I know, that was a long time ago but how does a store arrive at price tags starting at $1,299.99 and go beyond what a car or truck might cost.

During my shopping search I swear there had to have been five hundred various models, sizes, and colors to choose from, it was heart wrenching. It was just as challenging as the ordeal of choosing a wedding dress, I'm not kidding one bit.

The selection process was stunning, with cubic this and that to consider, decide on temperature-controlled crisper and meat storage, and single or dual cooling settings for doors. Choose between interchangeable or sliding shelves, and if you wanted micro-edge, frameless, glass, or metal shelves. I couldn't believe how many changes to a refrigerator had taken place over the years as if progress moved forward without my noticing.

Next, the shopper, me had to make a stunning decision, which model would best suit my lifestyle. I thought I knew what was needed in a refrigerator, I mean, I'd been in a kitchen since childhood, now I felt I was losing faith in my experience. Did I want the water dispenser inside or outside the door and should the ice maker be on the right or left side? Just as trying, where did I want the freezer? On top, bottom, or select a side freezer. See what I mean.

The choice to get a refrigerator with fewer amenities would have cost less, but none of those models were listed as being more energy efficient. See the guilt put on the buyer? I certainly wanted to do my part for ecology's sake, but the cheaper models didn't have a water dispenser or an ice-maker, which was a downer. Now I see how other countries look at us as spoiled. We don't even want the chore of freezing our own ice. Well, we Americans do drink a lot of iced tea, especially in the south where ice is considered real important in drinks.

The absolute worst thing that happened after buying a refrigerator, it would not fit where the old one stood. Obviously, manufacturers have decided big is the thing and are now making refrigerators way larger than they did a few years ago. So, a carpenter had to be hired to move a wall section to expand the space six inches, refinish with sheetrock, and paint. While that was being done the refrigerator had to sit in the dining room, inconvenient isn't the word to describe that two-week ordeal.

In addition to the new wall expense I had to purchase an extended warranty, the manufacturer will only guarantee the appliance for one year; I couldn't believe it! Apparently, refrigerator making companies don't put a lot of faith in the product they are producing. Just as astounding, a handling fee was added for delivery and set up. What! I spend money in their store then they charge a fee to deliver it; I tell you what, everyone has their hand out.

My old refrigerator gave me twenty years of cool service, survived my children, their friends and visiting friends and family; which was a lot of door openings. It didn't have a temperature-controlled crisper, a climate setting, or water dispenser, and I had to defrost the top freezer myself. Miraculously, it served a family well and survived a house-full of teenagers who stood at the opened door for what seemed fifty times a day. There is no other way to look at this as anything short of divine intervention, and might I add, it never once needed a single repair.

Now my biggest fear; another major appliance might "bite the dust". While looking at refrigerators I noticed how large washers and dryers are now days. They are huge, along with the price tag. A closer look revealed they are completely computerized. That is just frightening for someone not immersed in the world of computers and talking appliances.

I learned the new washers and dryers are controlled by a computer system to select the correct water temperature for what's being washed, soap and fabric softener is pre-computed, eco-boost is computed to save energy, and an app is offered so you can begin washing clothes while away from home. One simply makes a few selections on their mobile phone app and the washer begins its wash cycle. I suppose there is a magical robot from somewhere in the farthest reaches of the universe that connects to your washing machine start button, and with some high- tech hocus-pocus the washer begins washing the clothes.

Oh, my stars, I pray my existing washer and dryer out-live me!

I'm Walking the Floor Over
My Cowboy Boots

This may sound like nonsense to you, but I'm worried about cowboy boots. Truly, I am. When you learn what I've discovered, you'll understand the concern. The point is, in my opinion, anyone who wears and loves cowboy boots should know this.

Most cowboy boots sold today are not made in the USA. I'm serious, the Chinese are making them! I didn't discover this from a documentary; this awakening comes from weeks of searching for an ordinary pair of everyday cowboy boots. The existing boots I've had some twenty years were just plain worn out, so I began a search for a replacement pair.

Maybe I'm picky, or difficult to please, but I found nothing suitable made in America, I couldn't believe it. This was a jolting and exasperating revelation. I thought my search would be easy when I set out to buy a new pair of boots, it wasn't. I went to two western wear stores, several feed and ranch stores, then to a department store. Finally trying my hand at on-line sites, which is something I'm not good at, and still I came up empty-handed.

Sadly, I recognized brands once made in the USA that were now labeled, "Made in China". This didn't look good. I was simply baffled that millions of pairs of our sacred western treasure are being made in China, which I find disheartening. I mean, what do the Chinese know about cowboy boots? But here I was, faced with the possibility of never finding American-made boots. Still I kept looking. This is a common female characteristic completely misunderstood by the male species.

For some obscure reason, some men never think about things like shopping around until the perfect item is found, they simply don't understand, don't ask me why. I'm not an expert in much of anything, but I'd like to know how Chinese companies came to be making our boots? And puzzling still, why did it take me weeks to find boots made in America? Thank goodness I finally did, for there were times I believed I never would.

Anyhow, the shopping experience left me edgy and skeptical but thank goodness my search ended. Unbeknown to me, just down the highway was a wonderful ranch store that had hundreds of pairs of American-made boots. I was beyond a hallelujah happy to find exactly what I wanted. A plain, basic pair, soft leather, lightweight, a perfect fit and made in the USA. I was ecstatic, my family and friends heaved a sigh of relief to finally hear an end to my whining and complaining over the hunt for American-made cowboy boots.

But this troubles me. Apparently, as proven, the Chinese can make anything cheaper by using under-paid help. However, it's crossed my mind that a few items made there may not be quite perfect, or top-notch high quality, which I believed coined the throw-away society attitude. But I'm rather patriotic when it comes to cowboy boots; they are legends and should be made in the USA.

I mean, honestly, if John Wayne were still with us, what would he do? I'm willing to bet he'd be mortified at this discovery, possibly set out on a search like mine, complaining with words similar to "Pilgrim, this just ain't right". Still I'm worried about the future of a true American icon and confess to being somewhat irritated about this because I might want another pair of boots in a few years. Now I'm worried about what I'll have to endure by then.

And I'm worried about us, we Americans who love, and cling on to, our legends. To know real cowboys and cowgirls, urban ones too, are walking around every day, going to rodeos, or dressing up for a dance wearing Chinese-made cowboy boots is distressing. Honestly, I don't mind if the Chinese make electronics and a zillion other items, but cowboy boots, please, that's almost sacrilegious.

So, I ask, what happened? Well, it's possible a few American workers don't do much tedious, fine leather work so their bosses found another way to get the job done. Or was it a greater need for a cheaper made product?

What Is That Noise?

"What is that noise"? Whatever it is, it's downright annoying and scratches at nerves until they are raw! Ongoing, everyday ear-splitting crashing, crunching sounds are getting ridiculously louder, fraying nerves to the point of pushing one to grouchiness. Obnoxious honking horns, car mufflers, and street repair machinery blares continually, and it's getting worse with each passing week. Really!

Motorcyclists propelled with what sounds like gunpowder, not gasoline, accelerating to such speeds they appear as if attempting to break the sound barrier. Package delivery trucks bouncing down the street with stop after stop of screeching tires, cement trucks clattering, oil tankers rumbling and rushing everywhere continually fill the day with irritating booming noises. It's become madding to say the least.

People have begun talking loudly in libraries, remember that once quiet place! Some are shouting into cell phones in every available space we occupy, plus the odd and constant ring tones of phones is exasperating. And what is it with the way too loud music in the supermarket today? I feel as if I've entered a night club from yesteryear!

Weed eaters, chair-saws, and lawn mowers at very early hours were once only heard on weekends. Now their whine and roar fill's every day with an aggravating, deafening buzz. Garbage trucks arrive at the crack of dawn groaning, grinding, and crunching to disturb our early morning sleep. Piercing car alarms, blaring radios, fire, police, and ambulance sirens, thundering helicopters overhead, along with dogs barking, and roofers hammering from morning 'til night, have become daily, acceptable din. It's as if the world has gone deaf.

Video game sounds fill every space with millions of acoustic units of jargon for hours on end. TV commercials and infomercials are senselessly loud with non-stop chattering, some actually shout out the benefits of their products. Garbage disposals grinding and sputtering, dishwashers humming, washers and dryers thumping, the dull bang of the furnace heat or air conditioning kicking in are distressing interferences we contend with every day.

These sounds annoy me beyond description, moving my thoughts to dream of living in a remote area untouched by technology, the quiet would be heavenly, a step back to calm. I'm just plain sick and tired of security systems beeping, computers talking to us, news of doom and disaster on the television, and phones constantly beckoning us with strange musical note sounds.

We seem surrounded by perpetual chaos from incessant distractions of modern technology in every place we step. Somewhere along the way we have exchanged communication with the world and automatic everything for the disappearance of peace and quiet.

And why am I complaining about noise? Recently I went to see a remake of one of my all-time favorite movies. I should probably say right here and now, it was a mistake, a top-notch blunder that has led me to make a pledge; I won't be going back to a movie theater anytime soon. Within minutes Hollywood shredded my memories of my hero. The story was thoughtlessly changed. The noise deafening to the point I stuffed tissue in my ears and covered them with my hands in an attempt to close out the constant ear-shattering explosions that had nothing to do with the story I once knew.

My nerves shredded, nearly deaf, my ears ringing, and a beginning smack of a headache from the thunderous racket, I left the theater before the movie finished. I couldn't take it any longer. Sadly, only a few patrons appeared to be troubled by the overly loud noise and left the theater along with me because of the non-stop exploding, blaring sounds disguised as music.

The following day I discussed the ear-piercing incident with a nurse friend, learning I wasn't alone with my complaint. She said the increased noise in our daily life is getting louder, more frequent, and affecting more people. She added it's not just the older generations, young students are being diagnosed with hearing loss every day. They are experiencing hearing loss from loud sounds associated with video games, computers, and the movies they are constantly plugged into.

This confirms what doctors are discovering about the encroaching noise levels in our lives, booming decibels never seen before that are damaging young ears. Everyday loud noises are in our home, workplace, and where we play, reaching the point that they contribute to hearing loss and anxiety for millions. Doctors have also warned this type of non-stop racket can be unhealthy and interfere with our peace of mind. No kidding!

What happened to the quiet times, silence in certain settings, and tranquil places? Even our once peaceful parks are filled with noise. No wonder so many of us suffer from

146

insomnia and scattered thought because there isn't any quiet time left day or night!

Me, I'm giving thought to purchasing a pair of those ear protectors worn at the NASCAR race tracks because I'm fearful for my future hearing ability. Just as scary, my most frequent questions might become, "Could you repeat that", or "Huh?"

Lost In Space

A report from the FBI, the big brother snooper organization watching from everywhere, tells us we're losers! According to them we spend ten minutes each day, every day of the year looking for lost and misplaced items. Apparently, they know this from those observant satellite cameras in space photographing us losing stuff. That may or may not be true but at least we give it thought and ask how can they possibly know so much.

They tell us our losing habits are at the point of epidemic proportions, losing more and more as time passes pushing us to an irreversible stage. This is a very scary warning. Although, a finger should be pointed at the government for they lose just as much, if not more stuff than we do. Really. Oddly enough, most of the things they lose aren't found out about for years.

They're guilty of losing secret and classified documents, money, airplanes, ships, spacecraft parts, and tons of equipment labeled surplus. Somehow, it simply disappears without a trace! How can that happen, but just as questionable, shouldn't that classify them as losers too. Kind of like the kettle calling the pot black isn't it?

The thing is, the FBI is probably right when you look at what we as a people lose, it's staggering. How many mobile phones, eyeglasses, keys, wallets, TV remotes, or umbrellas have each of us personally lost? How many of us have been lost in the cyber world to the point where we vow to give up computers? Multiply our losing all sorts of things around the home by the millions of things lost daily and you realize the FBI is telling the truth, which in itself is difficult to comprehend considering their reputation for not telling the truth.

When we consider the money we've lost, bank cards, cameras, luggage, laptops, flashlights, and screwdrivers, we truly do appear to be losers. We are careless, absent-minded, and shameless, well we are. Ask anyone who has been to a lake, pool, or beach to count the number of flip-flops, beach chairs, towels, pairs of sunglasses, or tubes of sunscreen they have lost, all vanished into thin air. See.

We've all lost a hat, coat or jacket, and books at some point, we've each lost important papers, a parking space because we didn't move fast enough, and a lot of us have lost out on a promotion at work. Some, during our stupid years, lost our dignity, then after having children shouted out on numerous occasions, "I've lost my mind".

One of our problems is not locking things up so naturally they just disappear, lost forever treasures, jewelry, guns, automobiles, and tech and music equipment. Sport teams lose games, gamblers lose at card games, bingo, horse racing, and the lottery; this really does make us look and sound like a bunch of losers.

And what about people who get lost, some trying to get from one highway to another without correct directions, some sincerely want to disappear, and do. Every law enforcement agency loses track of criminals, con people, and regular citizens who simply disappear. Of course, there are all sorts of valid reasons, excuses that fill books and news articles with how and why so many vanish. Half the accounts are true, some are fabricated, and others are suspect they are now out of this world.

Quite a few of us, including myself, have accused Alien visitors of taking electronic devices, garage door openers, wine openers, scissors, files, and clothing that simply vanishes and is never found. It's entirely possible if these accusations are true then other-worldly beings are shop-lifting by picking up a few souvenirs from various places they stop. Well, it's not really a far-fetched assumption when an attempt is made to explain how so much of our stuff can simply disappear.

It's a given that we will lose our hair, figure, and maybe some weight; but worse, far too many have lost their common sense and thrown integrity out the door. It isn't as if we are surrounded by a Bermuda triangle concept, but to add up what we lose is unsettling, forever questioning where it went. I'd love to be able to say I've found half of the things I've lost, but I have not, which only adds to the validity of that FBI report. Humans are a losing species, period!

All of us have felt like a losing kind of person at some point. Most of us have lost a job, our vehicle to an accident, and furniture during a move. We get lost in the dark in places we are familiar with, lost in snowstorms, or have taken wrong turns trying to follow sketchy directions and gotten lost in places that scare us. But one of the worst is getting lost trying to take the shortcut to save ten minutes or ten miles and wind up getting so turned around we feel stupid.

Unfortunately, the FBI doesn't report the great joy we experience losing a marshmallow in a campfire, losing all track of time while frolicking on vacation, or losing a day or two because we've finally retired after years of work.

But there comes a time to put losing guilt aside, celebrate the sense of wonder we can know when the value of who and what we keep is realized.

Don't Mess with Our Avocados

Food distribution companies are reeling from shock over this unbelievable cowardly crime. A California sheriff's department has confirmed three produce company workers have been arrested for grand theft avocado. That's the honest to God charge! I'm serious! It was in print and on the internet. Seems these scoundrels were arrested for theft of up to $300,000.00 worth of avocados.

It's hard to believe anyone would even think of stealing our treasured avocados, but they did! Truckloads of them. Thankfully, the diligent deputies and detectives' working day and night to find the thiefs, the crooks were caught and arrested before they made off with any more. Can you imagine the suffering avocado lovers and guacamole addicts would have endured if these crooks hadn't been caught!

Seriously, this situation bordered on the unimaginable. Millions of supermarket shoppers, restaurants, and people from every walk of life should be forever grateful this horrific atrocity was crushed. Thousands are thrilled now that not one avocado loving person will have to be giving up those coveted, yummy avocados or go without spicy, mouthwatering guacamole.

The thought of not being able to eat a sandwich without avocado, enjoy crab or tuna stuffed avocados, anything avocado, would be difficult to comprehend or deal with. Think about this, there would be rioting in the streets and shadowy figures selling our tasty fruit on the black market. It could be similar to the gas shortage during the 1970s where people waited in line for hours, blaming the government, protesting. Those were horrible times.

Restaurants might be forced to close for lack of sandwiches piled high with luscious slices of ripe avocado or avocado salads; and heaven forbid we could not have guacamole. Restaurants would be desperate, bags of tortilla chips going stale on shelves; there's even the chance trucking companies would come to a standstill for lack of avocados to deliver. The industry could be changed forever, possibly triggering an economic bust.

Even the cheeriest consumer would be worried. The whole system of the four food groups would have to be changed and people would be grappling with how to live without avocados. Jobs could be lost, and its possible strangers would approach us in parking lots selling our precious fruit for $10.00 each or buy three and get one half price!

Salads would become utilitarian with not a bite of scrumptious avocado in them. Eating Mexican food would be bland, uneventful, moving some to resort to traveling to Mexico for the incredible taste of this aristocratic fruit. They would be moved to risk buying bags of this precious commodity, smuggling avocados across the border in an effort to satisfy their longing for the savory delicacy that revolutionized the American restaurant menu.

Without this nutritious nourishment, the enjoyment of avocados, the rules of preparing lunches and dinners would be seriously altered. I mean please, the avocado has been with us for at least 10,000 years so it isn't some trendy food a celebrity chef dreamed up or something foodies discovered as a fad food.

It's simply not possible to imagine there could be a small group of people who don't love the taste of or relish the delicious pleasure from avocados. But for those who worship, covet, and devour on a regular basis, this dazzling green star makes a day better because we love its creamy, savory taste. So, the squashing of this theft is monumental news! All of us wish the culprits and their black-market buyers will be thrown in the slammer for years.

While confined in jail, not one spoonful of guacamole should pass over their taste buds, not a single avocado salad, or veggie avocado sandwich be allowed to touch their lips during their stay behind bars! That said, this should be a lesson to any villain who dares to attempt taking our avocados; you'll wind up in jail and if ever released, sent to any place avocado trees can't grow.

There are just some things that will irk the masses when it comes to a treasured food being taken from us, and that something is avocados. They are true magical goodness, an art form of creamy green seduction, yummy in any form; they give us a reason to eat and live.

Incompetence Isn't All Bad

There are interesting and important jobs in the world, difficult, demanding, mind draining, and ordinary. Unfortunately, after a job is completed, or even before its finished there seems to be someone grumbling and complaining. Something isn't suitable, the outcome isn't as expected, or the appearance is criticized. The amount of nit-picking, fault-finding, and unsettling displeasure with something or the other seems an all too common occurrence.

At times, finished work displeases or annoys those expecting perfection, so whining that the assigned task wasn't done correctly, standards were not met, is expected. An outbreak of furious words on how incompetence is growing among the wage earners seems to come freely, with reference made to lack of pride in work, and poor skills.

So, it comes as no surprise that disappointment will be ongoing in the belief that working men and women, along with various types of businesses, have become sloppy. Their performance lacks pride and enthusiasm for the assignment before them in the eyes of those judging the worker.

If serious thought is given to this issue maybe incompetence isn't all bad. I'm not condoning or supporting it; but consider this. Maybe this shortage of talent in some is a gift. All of us were not meant to be free of ineptness.

If everyone was an expert, we would not be as appreciative of a job well done. Think about this. If you hired someone to fix something in your home and the work was not satisfactory, or it didn't work after the repair, someone else would be called to complete the job. The first worker's incompetence created a job for someone else.

How many times have we ranted about drivers on our roadways being unqualified to be driving a vehicle? If they were capable and proficient, there would not be a single accident. This might result in auto body shops not having any work on repairs, insurance agents wouldn't be needed, and salespeople wouldn't be selling replacement vehicles. Either of these cases would put people out of work, which is not good for the economy.

Mull this over. If every home builder, plumber, appliance repairman, financial advisor, or banker did everything right we would have fewer jobs. Or, what if government employees did their job perfectly every time; there would be no need for others to right the mistakes they make. Seriously, some of us just aren't as capable as we like to believe, while others simply believe they are perfect at everything they do, which of course is puffed up fantasy.

I don't even want to think what would happen if every IRS employee was efficient and accurate, they wouldn't miss our mistakes on those confusing forms we're required to fill out, usually under duress. What if the IRS worker never, ever experienced some form of miscalculating during their working career? See, we need a few distracted, disorganized, or low skilled people here and there.

There are advantages to incompetence at every turn in life, often beyond our comprehending. A number of my family members have several levels of ineptitude, which on occasion have made me look pretty good. However, an example of my lacking skills occurred several years ago after booking a flight on an airplane.

Believing the instructions given were followed correctly, an attempt was made to check in for my flight. Due to my bungling, the booking was not finalized, resulting in my having no seat reserved on the flight because I had not paid for the ticket. Thankfully a competent airline employee found another flight for me and righted my error.

The airplane for which I botched the reservation had engine problems on takeoff and never left the airport. My newly booked flight, by a competent airline employee got me to my destination.

Take my word for it; incompetence in all of us will at one time or another pay off.

Travel Itinerary

There are good things and bad things about traveling, which is unsettling because traveling should be easy, fun, a happy and good experience. But for some reason before we begin and after returning, we, the traveler, often feel exhausted, sometimes confused in both body and mind to the point we're moved to ask if it was worth leaving for such an outing.

Nevertheless, we go for the great pleasure in being somewhere other than where we live. It's an adventure, a chance to reflect, kick back and rest, and the thought of idleness and hope for fun excites us. So, the masses set out to travel, take leave from their common, daily existence to try something diverse and pleasurable.

As soon as we are somewhere different, we frolic, rest, or run ourselves into a dither in our attempt to take it all in, catch the fun, enjoy the difference. Leaving home to travel to another place will afford us new sights, a chance to explore the unique or historical, and offer us merriment, rest, and memorable encounters.

Leaving one place for another to seek the different has been going on for centuries. However, for some reason, we're still not all that good at it. We seek out the intriguing, the magical to tease our senses, to cure our melancholy, or to fill us with the pleasure of knowing we tried something diverse and eventful.

And so, we set off for the unknown, the opposite and unique to get away from home. But often our choices, whether leaving for a day or an extended time, somehow turn into a series of tactical exercises. Or it becomes bothersome as what we face may be less than expected when we encounter so many choices for getting to and from. This type of confusion may set our nerves on edge before we even set off for somewhere else.

In hopes of leaving captivity behind we step away toward freedom and choose our mode for getting away. If we board an airplane it can turn into quite a nerve draining and costly expense. Not to mention the possibility of the embarrassment of the security search. However, deciding on traveling by automobile as opposed to flying can also be rather trying, but it has its upside when it comes to cost and the ability to sightsee along the way.

Traveling by train was once a great adventure but it isn't a practical choice for many travelers in America, it once was but that glory has faded drastically. American trains can be quite challenging with well documented delays that will surely unravel nerves. Unknown to a first-time train traveler, "on time" to the passenger is a completely different thing to train conductors.

Traveling across the US today by this old-style method on rails often makes for shabby accommodations and late arrivals to a destination. Derailments are common, floods or flash floods wash out bridges, and cattle crossing the rails are commonplace. A derailment might be caused by a messy accident caused by a speed-crazed driver believing he can beat the train to the tracks, even with red lights flashing and the barrier arms down at a crossing.

159

The result of metal and plastic meeting with iron will of course cause a delay and a change in plans that could take hours, days perhaps. Animals are known culprits for causing train accidents and delays for they often wander onto the rails both day and night. So, the advice for a train traveler is... be flexible with your schedule.

Taking a bus isn't what it used to be either and from my experience, not a good choice for traveling any distance. Actually, I'm one of thousands who could pass on a horror story that would deter even the hardiest, toughest traveler from boarding a bus to go more than five miles. Other than a sightseeing day tour, I personally cannot recommend boarding a long-distance bus ever again.

In spite of some bad experiences over the years, I'm a believer in the trial and error method of driving to a destination. I sincerely believe it to be okay to make a mistake here and there, such as getting lost. This is something easily done for many, even with the new GPS devices. Those devices are not Einstein and too often guide a driver in the wrong direction, some wind up in places one should not be with young children.

Seriously, a few of us are not considered good at directions. Other than experiencing a few snags in finding one's way, pray you never encounter animals dashing across the road mere feet from your vehicle. Or God forbid the frustrating and costly ordeal of a break-down, the trauma of an accident, or a flat tire when one is traveling in a forsaken place in a mountain or desert area that isn't close to anywhere.

An entire page of pros, cons, and woes could be written on hotels and motels. No matter where you stay, for a night or a week, something is bound to go wrong or turn into an annoying frustration, or a complaint of some sort. Keep in mind, the smart traveler always asks for a room at least five doors away from the elevator or ice and vending machines.

Then one should always be up to speed on ins and outs, dos and don'ts of rental cars, the delusions one might have, which includes the possibility of chance taking and frustrations. Finding the lights, defroster, and locks in an unfamiliar vehicle could have an effect on one's moods and driving skills, then the beginning of ranting and questions on where is the A/C or heat dial, and who would buy this car? Or the entire family might ask, in unison, what is that smell? Believing it was possible pigs might have been transported by the previous renter of the vehicle!

Of course, a traveler always has an alternative when it comes to motels and hotels, both have a history of leaving the visitor with mind-numbing experiences. A more satisfying answer to the unknowns of accommodation is practiced daily by those who rent or purchase a travel vehicle. These home-on-wheels vehicles come in various sizes, which should be selected carefully, to either drive or tow. All are equipped with sleeping and eating spaces, as well as a bathroom, but keep this in mind. Most have cramped and small spaces that aren't always comfortable for tall or large size people.

Keep in mind this is not a vehicle for the faint of heart. An absolute must to consider is the driving class offered for such a vehicle, backing up can be a task that might need hours of practice. Breakdowns of such a vehicle have been known to occur in far from home or remote places, obviously triggering a few foul words to fly regarding costly repairs and towing fees.

The point is, we're aware of the missteps, danger, and upsets that lurk when one leaves the comforts of home. Still we seek out the adventure, strangeness, and the get-away to somewhere other than home. However, after venturing anywhere, everyone I know who leaves home, returns to make this statement, "It's great to be home".

Need A Little Help?

Finding someone to lend a hand, do a chore one cannot do oneself was once easily achieved. Today, it is near impossible to find a helping hand, those with talent and a strong back to assist with tasks we our self can't do.

Lucky us, for there are service companies readily available to repair just about anything. A roof, an automobile, or prepare our taxes, cut the grass, or repair a broken fence. If we are seeking to fix a smaller task such as a squeaky door, a leak in a gutter, or the strength to carry away an item no longer needed, few helpers can be found.

It appears those jobs are too small to bother the local handyman with, still it may mean a wait of three months or longer if used. Those with skills of an important nature are in high demand and often not available without a wait. Unfortunately, there are a few cheats waiting for the untalented to call and they will readily attempt to repair anything no longer working and charge an inflated price, even if the skill is not one mastered.

Finding someone willing to dig a hole for planting anything, trim a bush making a ghostly sound scratching a window, or to transport us somewhere when a need arises has become quite difficult. If a minor item around the house is too challenging, or the idea of attempting a repair brings on thoughts of failure or fear, we seek those who have more talent than our self. However, finding a willing, helpful soul nowadays can become a chore itself.

Turning to countless advertisements in search of those with skills in maintaining a home is imperative for those who lack ability in such tasks. We realize such artistry for repairing plumbing, electrical, or a broken appliance is best left to the trained and confident. But if locked out of our home or vehicle, this seems to happen quite often, the task of undoing the lock should not be attempted by the ill-equipped. A trained individual with a lock service to remedy this may actually be less costly than if taken on by the amateur, which is the person locked out.

When something of importance needs to be done at once, we are sometimes moved to call on friends and family. This may not prove to be ideal for they're probably just as untrained in this type work as we are, or busy at work doing what they do for a steady paycheck. So, shifting anything from our shoulders to another's isn't always a workable idea either; this could put us in a desperate state forcing us to leave tasks undone.

Delivery services are sometimes too slow and some are unreliable, while skilled manual labor drains our bank account, causes one to wait in line, then sometimes leaves us disappointed with the outcome. Domestic help has nearly vanished from existence. Finding those with needed skills to help us make it through a week, have found more pleasing work. So there again, finding someone to offer a hand has burdened us with constant shifting of chores, and most likely suffering the burden of finding our own taxi in the worst of weather.

If one should be plagued with field and forest creatures seeking refuge in an attic, there is a service company who will remedy that. This too happens more often than we think, but getting anyone to respond immediately isn't likely; therefore, one should be prepared for unknown creatures temporarily making themselves at home with you.

However, it is not recommended for the homeowner to venture into an attic to remove outdoor creatures. This could result in consequences one is not prepared to deal with, especially if the furry creatures resent your intrusion into their warm refuge. So, it should be pointed out that this is not a chore a homeowner should take on. Such an encounter may even add significant costs to a home repair, or when medical attention is needed after such a gamble, which is often the case.

Sometimes we fail or feel unqualified when one doesn't have the proper tools or strength to mow or trim a lawn, wash windows, or paint; burdens that tax us in our attempt to complete a job in a timely fashion or professionally. If this is true, one should employ services from the well qualified, be it plumbing, electrical, home repairs, or laborers of talent, those who do chores well, work we once thought of doing our self, but should not.

And when we do find a helper to exert themselves, let us be grateful for and cherish them for their lending of hands, especially when they make right the repairs we have attempted. Bless them, praise and reward them, pay them well, and consider yourself lucky, for good Samaritans and talented workers with helping hands, traits necessary for survival, are beyond a treasure.

Most of all, thank the Lord for giving them such talent and bringing us great joy, thus making them one of life's fine and satisfying pleasures.

The Lawn

Every homeowner's dream is to have a healthy, lush lawn. Foremost to complete this dream requires a willingness to work, be fully dedicated, and have knowledge of lawn pros and cons for it truly is the partaking of hard work. Each spring, the American suburbanite passionately seeks to elevate their self-esteem and satisfaction by cultivating a magnificent lawn. Therein, the pursuit begins with uncountable hours of work and maintenance to reach one's goal of creating their masterpiece.

The hardy and optimistic set about preserving one's reputation as a neighbor and lawn savior. Since the ravages of winter created havoc, an intense effort must begin by lawn enthusiasts and homeowners to restore their lawn to summer perfection. To begin one must update, restore, and create a retreat for relaxing, a haven for parties, a playground for children and pets, and a place that will guarantee self-praise.

But it's very important to pay attention to the advice and tips to achieve a dream lawn by doing your homework. Newspapers and magazines are full of guidance on choosing the right grass, flowers, shrubs, and trees to suit one's lifestyle and location. A homeowner must also acquire the correct equipment and learn new breakthroughs to produce an outdoor haven.

To establish a disease free, carpet of green a homeowner must be prepared to spend a good deal of money to assure the property value holds steady. Monitor fertilizing of everything growing; treat the soil for various insects, snails, worms, and weeds. Watering on a timely basis to achieve one beautiful, healthy retreat is paramount. Also, a magnificent lawn must be fed properly; keep in mind feeding is different from fertilizing, although both are essential.

If the lawn is neglected, property values may fall, your neighbors will hate you, and constant nagging or arguing with your spouse could be an ongoing ordeal. If you fail to work continually at maintaining the lawn, according to every gardening book printed, it will die; your life will change dramatically, possibly for the worst.

To save your lawn from certain death, you must purchase the right tools. Gardening tools, supreme possessions for a homeowner are like no other ownership of objects. Collecting an assortment of tools and gardening paraphernalia is fundamental to attaining a dream lawn, arranging a space to store said tools is just as important too. Storage of tools is essential, for if left in the elements they could be lost or deteriorate. After tools are acquired, one must invest in the most vital piece of equipment in your arsenal, the mower.

Depending on the size of the lawn, a mower could take up an area equal to a small car in the garage, unless you build a shed, or storage building, which could cost a sizable sum. This means a family discussion, or fuss, will take place as to where on the property the storage building, or shed, will be erected. After the mower has been purchased, another must-buy item will be the weed eater.

Weed eaters have become the most coveted of lawn tools, until they break, then they become the most hated and thrown away of instruments in your stash. Other items to add to your collection might include a leaf blower, shovels, rakes, clippers, trowels, pruning shears, ladders and fertilizer spreader. Garden hoses of various types and lengths are also vital; unfortunately, they are easily destroyed, usually cut in half by the lawn mower or left out during winter months when they freeze and burst.

Once armed with the proper, needed tools, hoses, and the mower, appropriate care is a requirement in order to preserve your equipment. This might require reading dozens of instruction manuals or taking a class on maintenance at a local college. Replacing belts, lubricating parts, and other grueling repairs are absolutely necessary. While cleaning and maintaining tools, make sure children are not within earshot because jarring words may slip out that youngsters should not be hearing.

Anyone can have a perfect lawn, provided enough money has been spent and the mind has been trained to spend approximately eight hours every weekend edging the walkway and driveway. Perfection can be achieved too by edging and trimming each shrub, every flower bed, and along every foot of fencing, each and every week. Also, keeping up with mulching leaves and assorted trimming, then bagging them for recycling. Keep in mind disaster will strike if the watering schedule is disrupted, so put that at the top of the list.

But what the hey… it's the lawn.

Smart Drivers

According to a national organization for senior citizens, driving has changed. So have our vehicles, traffic rules, driving conditions, and roads. Most of us know this but didn't pay it a lot of attention and now it's in the news as a warning to senior drivers. Seriously, well, apparently, the licensing czars of each state feel seniors might need a bit of prompting to update their driving skills. I'm not sure I agree.

Authorities, who appear to be the experts, say seniors should consider enrolling in the new driving classes offered free to all aged fifty and older. The classes are set up to test one's reflexes, new changes, tackle or overcome challenges in our computerized vehicles, and face the newest updates made to roadways, signage, and rules of the road.

The course will instruct drivers on how to adjust to challenges older minds and bodies might encounter, as they age, which prepares them for the driving environment we find our self in today. Students will learn safe and defensive techniques for traveling on streamlined highways, how to safely avoid unsafe drivers on the same road, and how to better operate high tech and computer guided modern vehicles.

The class is advertised as the Smart Driver Course, which sounds a bit confusing. Does this mean older drivers enrolled in the class aren't considered smart, but will be after taking the class; or does it imply graduates will be the smartest drivers on our roadways? The class also promises to help older drivers become less forgetful of their driving skills. This would be a God-send for seniors who have issues with remembering details. However, shouldn't this class be offered to frazzled moms, sleep deprived workers, and teens? All seem to have difficulty with summoning up a host of necessities required to get through a day, especially if embarking on any roadway or street.

During the past forty years senior drivers have become quite tough, experienced, cautious, and street wise, as well as having enough commonsense to spread around to a few youngsters who are less aware. So, it's rather amusing to learn other topics covered in the class will include how to follow a vehicle safely and manage age-related changes in vision and hearing.

Oh please. Seniors have the best insurance out there; as a result, they wear superior, updated eye ware, or have surgically implanted vision boosters allowing them great depth perception. And, their hearing devices are the most technically advanced available, they actually hear better than their teen grandchild.

Seriously, it's the younger drivers who can't see or hear. They constantly look at mobile phones, talking and texting instead of looking at the road at the same time they're listening to extremely loud music. They have been plugged into ear-splitting video games and music devices half their life, which means they are the ones that can't hear! Trust me; I've witnessed this first-hand, and so have doctors.

A number of younger drivers appear to have an entirely different set of rules for driving. They don't seem to follow guidelines for speed, are constantly on mobile devices or eating a fast food meal while steering the vehicle with an elbow or knee! Nor do they have any idea what a safe distance is, slamming on brakes right before they are inches from the vehicle in front of them.

It also appears that younger drivers tend to skip reading the driver's education manual, some never passing the driver's ED test but drive anyhow. And, statistics show some foreign drivers have not taken the test either. This means the cautious, seasoned senior driver must continually maneuver around those who have no idea what the rules outlined in a driving manual are.

Being a senior myself, I believe we are the better educated in every driving condition, including defensive driving. Seniors are on the alert to dodge those who exceed speed limits or who never use a turn signal, and they stay clear of those darting in and around vehicles that exceed the speed limit as if they are being pursued by the devil, or possibly practicing to enter a NASCAR race!

I personally believe senior drivers are on the defensive each time they leave home, intent on getting from one place to another safely. They plan on upping the ante for reaching their life expectancy age by being alert and cautious, knowing that crazed, unaware drivers are out there daily.

So, my question; why would seniors need this smart course? Seniors have better judgement and more common sense than the younger generation, who prove to us daily that they don't have much of either. Maybe I'm wrong; maybe careless driving is a form of entertainment to some, which in all possibility, and hopefully, is preparing them to become excellent senior drivers.

Waiting

I feel I'm as good at waiting as anyone, although, I tend to get impatient and a little annoyed if I am forced to wait longer than what is considered a reasonable time. This confirms I'll never acquire tickets to a popular rock band concert if the required waiting time took eight to twelve hours in line.

Waiting for a repair person to show up on time or within thirty minutes of a scheduled appointment should be a normal expectation. But to wait six hours for them to show up is just wrong, borders on inexcusable rudeness, and to be truthful, it's outrageous. That is, unless they call to say there has been a serious emergency and the appointment will have to be rescheduled.

When someone doesn't show up at a set time, arriving hours later is downright inconsiderate and rude. If they know they'll be late its common courtesy to call, give a worthy excuse or reschedule. But this doesn't seem to happen often enough because people who are notoriously late for nearly everything appear to be telling us, "Hey, your time isn't worth a flip and I can show up whenever I get around to it".

I don't mean to sound like an impatient person, but I've waited in doctors' waiting rooms for what seems like hours and in an emergency room for so long I began to feel my life was in jeopardy as I was bleeding more than I felt was normal. Seriously, how much time is allowed for bleeding before a staff person declares a doctor should be called now that you've bled out a pint of blood! That's something I've personally experienced.

Or, what length of time does the doctor's office staff say is long enough when the patient before them is writhing in pain? Should the patient be lying on the floor, screaming and moaning before the nurse/assistant, calmly says, "The doctor will see you now."

I'm not one to show up late for anything unless there is a serious traffic or weather condition that suddenly happens while I'm en route to where I'm scheduled to be. So why is it that some people think they can just waltz into an appointment whenever they feel like it, believing the person waiting for them has all the time in the world, or thrilled by the opportunity to be in their presence?

And why does a company or person expect, actually believe it's okay, for several dozen people to stand in a line for an hour when there is only one person at the help window? This should be motivation for a call to hire another staff person to help handle dozens of people who are forced to spend half a day waiting. And this is beyond ridiculous; when asking a person in a store for something, they leave and don't come back for twenty minutes to tell us, "We don't carry that item any longer". Shouldn't they have known that if they work there?

Waiting at a restaurant for more an hour to be seated can also be unnerving, but once seated it seems to take half hour for the waiter to arrive. Once the food is placed before you the waiter disappears again. Sometimes I believe the staff purposely ignores us to get even with their management who they are at odds with. Well that excuse is as good as any; or it's possible the restaurant ran out of food and had to send out for it! This has really happened more often than we want to believe.

In my opinion, one of modern man's most annoying chores is waiting. It can make the waiting person jittery, worried, or hopping mad. For myself, being on time is a courtesy but waiting and waiting is something I'm not good at. Maybe I have a fidgety personality or maybe I'm too polite, for if I say I'm going to be somewhere at ten o'clock, I'm usually there five minutes early.

Waiting is an unavoidable experience if you want to get or buy anything, go anywhere or make an appointment for anything. So, if you are an older person, be glad you have hung around long enough to wait for a person or something you will enjoy. Remember there is nothing beyond the grave! If you are younger, be grateful you have something to wait for, which was most likely provided or made possible by an older person.

Moral of this story... If you show up late, a lecture might be directed at you, or a simple quite politeness shown to where you know you are being written off as rude, but if you show up on time it will gratify some and astonish the rest. Or consider this, if you wait until you are absolutely sure you want to do something or see someone, it may be too late.

The National Society of Cheating

Cheating, double-crossing, and swindling of every description has been with us for eons, probably around the time one cave man stole another's meal, or his woman. So why is it that modern man's acts of stealing and cheating are a surprise? Taking another's possessions, cheating, stealing, extortion, and double-crossing their fellow man is a way of life for some, the norm as they say.

Today cheating appears to be a way to do business, the first steps to cultivating a friendship, run a government, or do almost anything. This type of sneaky, unscrupulous behavior is commonplace, going on each and every day across the world. The practices of bilking, taking from others, lying and betraying, are so prevalent, they've become a mastered skill. Which leads me to believe something is not quite right in the world. Crooks and cheaters are everywhere, including church, families, and the government. It's both scary and worrisome.

Seriously, some of us are just now catching on to a few unsavory practices that aren't as honest as they should be. People don't seem to be up front in everything done, practiced, or said. Controversy on where an item is made, what county, what is in it, and what it's really made with has most of us frightened and concerned.

Today it's common for people to lie and cheat in their business, their personal life, anything regarding clothing, jewelry, personals, their car, their actual job, and schooling background. It's become so difficult to trust that everyday

177

people seem to be participating. Low-life cheaters claim they have police training or have served in the military when this is not the case at all. They simply make up any lie they can think of that might enhance their bank account.

The government, which we would like to believe is nobody's fool, keeps doing things that cause us to believe it is, and quite good at cheating and lying. It has taken cheating to a whole new level the past few years, allowing deceit of every imaginable kind, cheating and juggling things to the point people may have forgotten what it hasn't cheated at.

Little by little, it adds up and catches up, and now the government is trillions and trillions of dollars in debt and can't even tell us exactly how much. Thousands of government employees in every branch and department have been cheating, stealing, lying, fixing the books, and double-crossing us for so many years it has become a regular way to conduct business at any level.

Even the IRS, the most famous of places to catch cheats, can't seem to catch up to all the con artists because the swindlers have become so good at it, it's now a profession. Cheating is an honest to God business, a way to behave, do business, and expect to get by with all types of bamboozling practices.

Over time, respectability has faded away and morality has gone out the window. More and more no longer consider it one's duty to be honest and straightforward up front with others; taking the attitude of everyone else is doing it, why not me? This is of real concern; somewhere right and wrong has been lost in the shuffling of values and needs, so cheating is an answer to those who put little value on the consequences of lost, non-existent, or never-known morals.

This is just as alarming and something to bear in mind. The business of cheating has never been more profitable, worth selling their souls to the devil because people are making a living at cheating, stealing, and worse. An excess of information is being shared among the dishonest so they can survive at this age-old lifestyle, keep out of jail, and continue to con the general, trusting, unaware public.

Companies are losing so much revenue due to employee stealing they are now secretly watching their staff at work, workplace spying. Employees are becoming dishonest, rather like taking up shoplifting of products, stealing money, customer credit cards, and more. Airport workers, even visitors to the airport, are stealing luggage, purses, briefcases, technical devices, cell phones, and more.

Computer hackers are making quite a headway in destroying and stealing information that will bring them more income. Vacation planners are renting property that doesn't exist and con men/women find all sorts of ways to cheat and con the vacationer, it's become similar to a contest of who can cheat the most.

Presidents and dictators of countries are notorious cheaters and liars. So are Senators and Members of Congress, many of whom have been practicing bamboozling and shifting the truth for decades. When caught at wrongdoing they apologize and insist they didn't know they had made a misstep.

So, where does this leave us? Scattered, surprised, disappointed at the flimflam reasoning for bad behavior. But this really sets my temper aflame when the receiver of cheating and lying has been harmed beyond repair. Wedding vows are not honored, the truth is not disclosed on things sold, some great stories are simply made up, a farce, and our ancestors real background appears tangled in a web of deceit and cheating to the point many have no idea who their relatives are.

Fleecing, trickery, cheating, whatever one wishes to call it gives reason to use the old tar and feather practice on cheaters who practice such acts of swindling their fellow man. At least when we were confronted, they could be avoid because of their feathers.

"Tis my opinion every man cheat's in his way, and he is only honest who is not discovered."
    - Susannah Centlivre

Can You Read the Small Print?

I have a gripe about the printed word. You know what I'm complaining about. The print on every bottle of medication the pharmacy has ever handed to me is unreadable. I'm not kidding, I can't read one word on the prescription bottle, I bet you can't either! I can't read the medication name, directions, how much to take, or the expiration date because the print is so small a 10x magnifying glass is needed to see it. Why is this?

The doctor's name, phone number, when the prescription can be refilled, and any warnings are printed so small they're almost a blur. Any possible adverse or allergic reactions can't be read, which is scary, nor can the name of the manufacturer be made out; they too are in such microscopic print nothing is readable by the human eye. No wonder most of us miss taking the correct dosage of medication on a timely basis. It's downright annoying.

Not one word of information printed in fourteen languages on a tiny slip of paper folded and placed in the drug store bag makes sense because the print is even smaller than the smallest printed information on the medication bottle. This print is so miniscule it's hopeless to try to read, even the one printed in English!

This statement in larger print should send chills down our spine; "Read Warning Signs and Possible Side Effects!" There again the warnings are so small they also need a magnifying glass to read, plus they take up the entire paper. This is more than unsettling because the person taking the medication should know what the warnings are up front, placed at the very top of the page. Another question I have, why is the language you are proficient in on the very last page, which is the one in English?

The whole ordeal of trying to read a medication label on your personal medicine bottle is annoying to millions and I do mean millions. Little if anything printed can be made out by the naked eye; how can they get by with this crap? We should know immediately how much to take or how often, how many pills to take at what times, is it one every two hours, or two every hour? It's maddening when you can't see the instructions without reading glasses, plus an added magnifying glass. This should be illegal!

I've reached an age, like my friends, where I need reading glasses to read anything, which I hate because they are never in the place I thought I left them. If I go shopping, I can't read the ingredients on a box or bottle of anything from crackers to shampoo!

If I want to read the label or price tag on anything in a store, I must search my purse or pocket for my reading classes. Instructions on anything being sold, or in what country the item is made, require glasses to read because there again the print is in such itsy-bitsy print you can't read it. Worse, I can't sit back to read a novel, work on a computer or iPad, do a crossword puzzle, or see playing cards without reading glasses.

Going out to eat requires I take my reading glasses because menus have been printed for Leprechauns. Although large colorful pictures of the food, displayed on the menu can help. I can't see phone numbers on business cards, or whose card I'm holding. Nor can I read who my mail is from, and notes left for me to call so-and-so also require me to don my glasses. I feel I've lost contact with everyday reality because I'm blind as a bat!

I know this is an age-related issue; still it's put me in such a bothersome place where if I ever want to see anything printed, or look up anything, I'll forever need those dang glasses. What will I do if I travel to an area where I can't get a signal for GPS? I'll never be able to find where I'm going, or where I'm at if I have the feeling I'm lost or on the wrong highway because maps are also in teeny-tiny print! This of course means I'll have to start a search for my reading glasses, if I can remember where they were last.

Reading is bliss, educational, a time out get-away; my entire life has depended on it for work and personal satisfaction because I love reading. Now I shop for books that are printed in large print because everything I want to read revolves around reading glasses!

Ahh, the age of wisdom is great, but the age where the eyes begin to fade is so uncool! Wearing reading glasses is not only bothersome; it's frustrating when they can't be located. By the way, I was once cool, really. But wearing reading glasses to see the D for putting my vehicle in motion is a perfect example of uncool!

Complaint Department

Why is everyone complaining? From the sound of things, it's epidemic! Grumbling and whining, blaming and criticizing someone or something, constantly. It's got to the point most of us hesitate to listen to, watch, or read the news for fear it will set us off and throw us into muttering nervousness. We're tired of strange people doing odd stuff, and of course sick of the accusing and fault-finding, most done with inaccurate accounting. If it isn't an individual, it's a group pointing fingers at, condemning, or scolding someone or something.

As a young girl I remember complaining because I had to wash dishes every day because my sister broke her wrist. Dishwashing was a shared task then, a take-turns agreement for either washing or drying and putting away. With her cast on for weeks I got stuck doing the dishes because she couldn't wash or dry. To me that was valid complaining. No, we didn't have a dishwasher!

Today my granddaughters complain or argue if they are assigned to help load or unload a dishwasher! And they fuss over where they ride in the car, left or right side and whine if they aren't getting enough air conditioning or heat. They whine and pout if they can't get a newer, more state-of-the-art electronic device or that new pair of boots, or go to an event that has ticket prices costing nearly as much as a new set of tires for a car. What happened?

America prospered. People went off to college, got better paying jobs, became spoiled, wanted more, expected more, and got more. Now they grumble about not having this or that, bemoan their city or state isn't doing enough to make their life easier, bewail that they aren't being provided with more; or they are fuming because of road construction.

Recently, even members of the Peace Corps were heard complaining. I thought they were a peaceful group! This constant condemnation and griping from so many ungrateful people moves me to believe it's only a matter of time before God reaches down and smacks some sense into them, or sends them into hell; they'll really have something to complain about then!

Come to think of it, he probably has smacked a few straight into hell. Anyone ever find out what happened to Jimmy Hoffa? Its possible God smacked him straight into hell for he was a bit of an unsavory character. I remember him on television shouting and accusing, featured on national news with stories that were unsettling, and hints of his dealings with criminals. He often appeared with a shaking of fist, threatening, complaining, sounding mean and hateful, and intimidating those around him. Then one day he simply disappeared, never to be seen again.

Have you ever wondered what really happened to the thousands of unsavory people and criminals who disappear every year? I'm not sure I believe the theory that they were kidnapped by Aliens or they escaped to Alaska, vanishing into the wilderness. It's quite possible God just quit trying to save them and sent them straight to Hades to give Satan a hand with stoking the fires.

No matter where we go or to what type of event, we hear complaining of every kind. Grumbling about lack of parking, the weather, high prices for water and electricity service, standing in line, people texting and eating while driving, at the same time speeding. It appears we have constant moaning about politicians and politics, robbery and mayhem, or grocery store prices; none of which will do much good.

Fuel prices, food prices, movie tickets, and prescription prices are expected to increase but complaining because your neighbor is driving a large vehicle that may pollute the air; please. Increasing prices for checked bags at the airport is to the point it drives people batty. My grandmother spoke of the difficult times during the Great War that tested everyone with rationing; maybe we should be grateful we don't have that to deal with, although, if the masses continue with ridiculous complaints, it's possible it could happen again.

Students complain they have too much homework, teachers grumble parents aren't helping enough with it, and the principal bemoans his pittance of a salary, while the superintendent demands more pay for the same work. I hear people complaining about their job, traffic, internet and everyday services. While at the movies over the weekend I was stunned to hear a woman complaining to the concession cashier her popcorn had un-popped kernels in it. Good grief, where will it end?

My cousin's complaints rank with the best of world whiners, creating a fuss about any and everything no matter the time or place. I truly believe her husband passed away from being nagged to death; then she had the nerve to moan and groan to the funeral home his casket wasn't the shade of gray she remembered ordering! She gripes the church pews are too hard, whines about food at every restaurant, and criticized the 4th of July decorations at City Hall. The woman doesn't seem to have a grateful bone in her body; maybe God should smack her into reality! See my point.

There is almost nothing, no matter how trivial, that the ridiculous thinking, the miserably unhappy, or bored won't venture to complain about, especially if they can find an audience. And therein lies the issue, no matter how much you explain, complainers will refuse to compromise on anything, forever critical of everything imaginable and unimaginable.

Consider this; try as we may, there will always be leaves stuck in the downspouts, we will at some time or another get a wicked cold the day before our vacation begins, and be left with cleaning up the mess from spilled milk. Even if we didn't spill it.

It's possible we could be quite moved by some very fine things if we would just turn around and look. Especially at morning sunrises, evening sunsets, and the stars in the heavens at night.

The Aluminum Foil Crisis

When I tumbled out of bed to a pleasant morning, I was thankful to have made it through the night, I felt great. Once up and about, reviving myself with coffee, surveying the house, happy to discover not one thing had sprung a leak, failed, or broken. I felt a lucky woman today. Then I turned on the television for the day's news.

A visibly shaken reporter was speaking about a serious issue facing the nation. The subject was a newly released report from a well-known medical advisor at a trusted research facility. The newscaster appeared in a flutter, her eyes glazed, her demeanor grim to where one couldn't help but listen. Still, I hesitated for as much as we hate to admit this, not everything is accurate because way too many reporters aren't telling the truth on national news today.

The announcement was regarding a health threat released to alert the public about a national threat. After years of research the results were in and now released as a warning for the public to be on guard. The threat? Aluminum foil is making us sick; that's right, the treasured invention we've cooked with and used for decades is gradually wiping us out.

I'm serious; or rather the news reporter was. Aluminum has seeped into our cooked food and homes, deemed suspect for causing unhealthy afflictions and complaints. The reporter wasn't exactly how this had happened, yet she was sure she was giving us enough information to put us on guard in case it is fact.

She continued on with the announcement the research team isn't completely sure about the suspected deadly outcome of using aluminum foil, or for that matter, anything aluminum, including cookware and products that may have a hint of aluminum in it.

As frightening as this sounds, baking a potato, or cooking a chicken, ham, or turkey encased in foil shouldn't be an unhealthy choice, but the experts are telling us it is, or that it could possibly be and we should all be on alert. This just doesn't sound as if they really know.

Which leads me to ask; why would they release a report of breaking news if it can't be verified as truth beyond truth. Just as scary, this couldn't have come at a worse time because this troubling announcement has hit just as the holidays are upon us. This means three-fourths of America's population may hesitate, or not cook at all holiday meals wrapped in aluminum foil.

Now I'm worried that once this report gets out, millions will be confused; how will we bake or cook anything, what will we line cookie sheets with, or cover picnic dishes? Men will be doubly perplexed, how can they grill outdoors, barbecue, or cook a rack of ribs without foil? How can we have a soft drink or beer? They are sealed in aluminum drink cans.

Just as frightening, we are surrounded by aluminum. Our windows, doors, electrical items, and more are made of this needed lightweight, durable metal. How will NASA deal with this? Parts of their spacecraft and the astronauts' suits are made using aluminum, plus the food taken into space is sealed in tiny plastic and aluminum packets. See, this is already creating so much confusion to the point that dozens of questions and doubts on how to manage without our precious metal have already reached the point it's become unsettling and quite bothersome.

Do you want to know what's wrong with America? Well I'll tell you; we have too many alarmists, studies, surveys, and experts, including news reporters that don't have their facts straight! Now some medical know it all comes along and tries to convince us we are being harmed by what seems an unexplainable phenomenon.

Researchers are just as guilty for they've reported foil will cause memory loss, thin our bones, and cause weight gain over the course of years of use. What a bunch of dingbats these so-called researchers appear to be, all this happens as we age; what an idiotic report! I'm willing to bet every one of those researchers in the study group is under the age of forty!

I have always been wary of news reports about what research people are doing. Needless to say, this released report sounds a little hokey, not good for the American public, especially cooks. I say we should challenge those experts, get a petition, seek legal counsel to address this craziness, have a court hearing, or whatever you do to get this report reversed.

So, here is what I'm doing. I'm going to risk it, I won't be oppressed, this is a free country and I'll use aluminum foil for anything I want. Rejoice in the fact I'm protected from the elements with my aluminum windows and doors, and I can sit comfortably in my aluminum lawn chair drinking from an aluminum can.

And, I truly believe NASA will call these researchers a bunch of scaremongers who want attention. It's also very possible those researchers didn't have much to do one day and decided to take a look at aluminum, believing there might be the possibility it could have some sort of adverse effect on the human body.

NASA will of course, continue on, most likely not worry at all because those aluminum food packets haven't made one astronaut sick yet, and they've been eating space food out of them since the 1960's; so there.

But, thank goodness I don't have to use foil on my TV antenna anymore.

Watts Up

There's a lot going on these days that doesn't make sense, buying a light bulb for one. I'm not kidding about this when I ask, have you bought a light bulb, any size, in the last year? Well, surprise, surprise. The light bulb industry has changed so much we now have somewhere near five-thousand types to choose from!

It's true, listen to this; there was once a time when we could walk into a store, buy a four pack of ordinary bulbs and that was it. Bulbs for ceiling lights, lamps, the porch, anyplace a light was needed. We can't do that today because finding the correct light bulb for dozens of types of light fixtures created over the past decade is so confusing, a Lighting Specialist employee will be called to assist you when you shop for any bulb. And, I kid you not, that is a valid title. I don't know what sort of training they go through, but it's got to be intense and those chosen for the job most likely will be the type with a lot of patience.

I will attempt to explain. All I needed was an appliance bulb for a five-year-old refrigerator; why it burned out is a mystery because the bulb in my mother's refrigerator lasted for twenty years. It's not as if there are three teenagers spending thirty minutes each, six times a day, holding open the refrigerator door, yelling, "There is nothing in here to eat.'' This would of course shorten the life of a bulb, but the children are grown and gone.

Fortunately, there are only six types of appliance bulbs, but to muddle the mind to the point of shock when bulb shopping there is somewhere near a zillion types of bulbs to light up everything, indoors or outdoors. It's possible that when the buyer sets out to buy a bulb it might help if one had a degree in electrical technology or carried a guessing charm blessed by a leprechaun.

Buying any bulb today is perplexing and difficult, mind altering, and no matter what your fixture is needed for or where the bulb socket is. Honestly, you will spend at least half an hour searching, with another half hour spent with a salesperson who is the Lighting Specialist the store has sent to assist you. The pathetic outcome is that you could still come away with the wrong bulb.

A shopper for any type of bulb will need to go armed with a bit of knowledge that includes the size, what shade of light, wattage, how many lumens, and is it a halogen or energy efficient is a must. To be successful in the purchase, according to the Lighting Specialist, you should know if an LED long life, cool or warm, natural daylight, bright, soft, or white light is required. This alone could cause the buyer to make a list and have light bulbs added to it: The Ten Most Mundane Things That Drove Me to Insanity. See what I mean.

Is the bulb for indoor or outdoor use? Almost everyone knows there is a huge difference; outdoor bulbs must be weather resistant and the buyer must have the expertise to determine if it's for motion, solar, high intensity, high pressure, multi vapor, or flood, and what watts or lumens will be needed for the size of space it lights. See how frustrating the search for a bulb can be?

This is needed too. Watts for bulbs range from 8.5 to 500, buying the wrong one could mean it might burst into flames. All this is rather exasperating for the buyer; so is the price charged for bulbs today. They may range from ninety-nine cents to $42.00 each! What is wrong with this? I remember buying a four pack of plain 100 or 60 watt bulbs for a dollar. I truly believe we as bulb buyers have been had!

It is possible bulb-making companies set out to confuse the masses, became greedy, and are now laughing at the new language they created, not to mention the new higher prices they came up with to increase their profit. That may not be exactly accurate, but it sounds as if capitalism might have a few flaws or else there are lighting engineers with too much time on their hands.

Our top priority is a light in the refrigerator; okay, the house, deck, patio, the barn, maybe the pool. However, we don't need everything to be lit up as bright as the solar system, but according to the electric bill, it is.

Lost and Found

I'm a losing kind of person I suppose you might say. It's part of who I am, but then, we're all considered losers at some level, so I don't feel singled out. To be precise, the world population is full of losers, seriously. Everyone loses all sorts of things every day, sadly, most of the things that are lost are never found.

However, the losing isn't as bad as the number of people with difficulty accepting they are losers. To be truthful, confessing to losing things is tough, especially if it happens often. There are personalities in denial for some reason over things they misplace; some simply lie about it, while others don't seem to be bothered. The rest are simply absentminded people who misplace or forget where they left things.

Some folks lose more than others. Me, I seem to lose a lot. Regular things, money, keys, sunglasses, at least a million ball point pens, dozens of socks in the dryer, and notes I write seem to vanish as if the paper dissolved like those secret coded message spies are said to use. I've lost important stuff too. My job, furniture during a move, my car to an accident, lost my dog, and sadly a few friends and family members have died, and even more hurtful, I lost the love of my life.

I'm not alone when it comes to losing; ordinary and famous people have been losing things since time began. Think about it, misplaced treasures, art, gold, ships, even planets, to name a few, have gone missing over the centuries. Some lost due to misguided planning or theft, poor directions or natural disasters, others from ridiculous or mindless acts of foolishness and stupidity. From these actions a lot of lost items were actually stolen and never found, considered lost.

Seriously, who lost, rather who was in charge when the Ark of the Covenant went missing in the sixth century? It's never been found! Kings and Queens, along with Dictators have lost whole countries, wars, crown jewels, even their dignity and legacy. I've personally lost items in my home over a period of decades, some were found, some not, all resulted in a few odd hunts. This was a good reason for teasing from family and friends, as well as accused of being absentminded. Thank goodness I didn't lose my dignity like Queen Mary.

Cell phones, TV remotes, garage door openers, books, files, and instructions for electronic devices in my home have simply vanished over the years. My kitchen is like a black hole, items and gadgets disappeared like a zigzagging spirit, simply vanish, never to be seen again. Garden tools have disappeared mysteriously as if they melted into the dirt and various small tools used in the home are just gone. Sewing and regular scissors, calculators, several staplers, and household screwdrivers have gone missing over the years, seemingly vanishing into the air as if they disintegrated.

This of course gives me thought; perhaps Alien invaders have taken my belongings over the course of my losing spree. If you consider all the lost things with a rational outlook, it's possible Alien beings like picking up souvenirs from various places they visit. When you lose as much as I have the mind does wander to varied possibilities, so accusing out of this world visitors isn't such a far-fetched assumption.

I've lost battery jumper cables I'd never used; I didn't know how to use them anyhow, and that unusual wrench which opened the hubcap so a tire could be changed simply disappeared from the trunk of my car. How do such things like that vanish without a trace? Especially items you knew were originally there but had never used.

And that odd tool that comes with every garbage disposal; you know the one I'm sure, its "L" shaped, about the length of a short pencil, always kept under the kitchen sink for it can't be used for anything else that I know of. Well, each and every one in every house I've lived in has disappeared, not one person in the house would ever admit they used it. Perhaps it might work on Alien spacecraft for restarting an engine, I mean, anything is possible. So, once again I point a finger at beings visiting from space; sounds like as good a guess as any.

As a child my mother said I lost stuff constantly, hats, gloves, coats. She punished me for losing things in an attempt to teach me to be more aware and respectful of my belongings. That didn't quite work because over the years I lost watches, jewelry, shoes, along with towels, snorkel masks, sunglasses, and sunscreen at the beach. I lost several suitcases by trusting them to the airlines, which wasn't my fault, still I lost them.

Another area relating to me personally, a fault of mine I've lived with for years, could honestly declare me directionally challenged. It's been difficult over the years to admit, but I've been lost so many times I don't dare remember. I've had numerous scary experiences and way too many nitwit thinking wrong turns, embarrassing situations that brought me to tears.

Getting lost in a foreign country where I did not speak the language was such a frightening ordeal that I was close to shock. However, I did find my way and the trip ended well. This should give those of us who don't follow directions well a bit of hope, there are caring people the world over who are willing to help get you back to the correct road. In one case, yes there were several situations during my travels afar. A local policeman took pity on a lost American in his country and helped me find my way back to the hotel. Unbelievable as this may sound; I couldn't even pronounce the name of the hotel.

I've never been good at directions, reading maps, or locating landmarks, which might identify me as a failure at finding the way in unfamiliar places, especially after dark. I'm not good at puzzles or scavenger hunt games either. I'm certain I could never have qualified as a navigator with NASA's exploration team, most likely I'd have gotten the entire crew lost in space had I been put in charge of directions to get us home.

I've lost quite a few umbrellas too, some while traveling across six countries, dozens of cities, and vacation spots. Plus, I'm terrible at card games, so I lose there too, I'm not that good at sports so I've lost at that as well. However, everything I tried and lost at was at least fun. Although, I once lost my wallet; it was as if an apocalyptic scenario had begun, thinking my life was over. Thank God and an honest woman, it was returned.

The good news, I've found a few things too, some interesting and rewarding. I've picked up nearly a million pennies I hoped might bring me luck. I stumbled across several dollar bills found lying on the ground like they were thrown away candy wrappers, I picked them up. Quite some time back

I found a puffy envelope beside a trash bin at a casino, no one was around so I looked inside, I discovered several hundred dollars wadded up. It was just lying on the floor by a bunch of trash strew around, apparently accidently thrown away so I kept it.

I once stepped on a hundred-dollar bill in the parking lot at my bank. Looking around not a soul was to be seen. I asked inside the bank if anyone had lost money on the way out to their car, not one murmur. So, I kept it. Another find was a paper sack on the floor of my office building elevator. Thinking it was lunch trash, I planned to throw it in the garbage bin; it was so heavy and clinked of metal, I peeked inside. It was full of quarters, $44.00 to be exact. I waited two weeks for someone to claim it; no one did so I kept it too.

A necklace bought at a yard sale for fifty cents was actually 14k gold, and the intriguing things purchased at flea markets for next to nothing became interesting and profitable finds. The most rewarding was a book found at an estate sale for a dollar. When I spoke of it to a friend, he advised me to take it to a bookstore specializing in old and rare books. The price they offered was a windfall for me. Seems it was a first edition, printed in 1805 and quite rare.

I'm not a dumpster diver but I found a small, tossed away painting laying on top of my neighbor's trashcan after they moved. The picture was in plain sight at curbside, obviously thrown away. I sold it to a gallery; it was an original worth a fortune, well it was a jackpot amount to me.

I don't lose as much as I once did; I believe I've become more mindful for the one thing I never want to lose is who I am.

I'm holding on pretty well and it's interesting how life can alter that part of one's self. Losing trust in those believed in has been difficult to accept. Still, I have faith I'll not lose my trust in everyone and won't let a storm ruin my parade.

So, the lesson of losing might read: Lose a little, lose a lot, you feel sad, sometimes dumb; but finding something beloved, rewarding and profitable you feel happy, lucky. But to discover the best pizza place in town is a lucky deal, finding out who your real friends are and who truly loves you is a treasure, the best finds on earth.

Elevators, the Up and Down of Trust

I don't trust elevators and only use one if it's necessary, they're simply not a place I'm comfortable in. Unfortunately, most who ride an elevator have at some time hesitated to step into one, which sounds like a phobia to me. Which I believe I have, and if I do it's mixed in with my claustrophobia label as I hesitate going into tunnels, buildings I can't see a quick way out of, and get the willy-nillys if I have to take an elevator. Seriously, I've been quite wary of elevators for some time, or lifts as my British friends refer to them.

When I was child, I loved riding in the one and only elevator in my small hometown. From the age of five until my teen years my mother took me shopping in the department store that included three floors of goods. There we shopped for clothing, shoes, bedding and kitchen wares, cosmetics, and personal items and always took the elevator to the second floors. We stepped onto an elevator where a lady attendant sat in front of a brass panel with numbers 1, 2, and 3, we thought of the ride a treat, almost magical.

She closed the folding door by moving a large metal handle, and then pushed a button; the elevator moved slowly up or down. Within minutes, we could step out onto a completely different floor to shop. When my cousins and friends were about twelve, we would ride the elevator just for fun, sometimes going up and down two or three times until the attendant made us get off.

During my youthful working years, I rode a crowded elevator to my office, always with the feeling of being closed in, becoming uncomfortable and edgy as time passed. A new job had me in a downtown office building on the twenty-second floor. This meant I would ride shoulder to shoulder with dozens of workers going to offices. I became more squeamish as time passed.

If there were odd sounds of creaking, grinding, or the car was too full; people made noises of concern and some would get off to take the stairs, which usually included me, so I wasn't alone with my concern. Over the months the elevators seemed to make more odd noises as if the aging car was finally wearing out, which made me become more wary of elevators.

And then it happened. One freezing winter morning I planned to arrive early to work, finish important assignments and leave quickly as weather predictions for late afternoon were grim. On that morning, in that building I experienced every nightmare that could be imagined with an aging elevator, the incident gave me a reason to change jobs.

Arriving at the building, discovering two co-workers had the same plans; leave before foul weather would make driving home difficult. Once inside the elevator, moving toward our office, the elevator groaned and jerked to a stop, alarm sounds rang out; sirens were heard in the distance, I froze in place. The first thought was oh, no, the wretched thing has finally broken.

The elevator shuddered to a stop-thud between the 7th and 8th floor. Within seconds, the faint smell of smoke produced an uh-oh from all three passengers. The building was on fire! The elevator had automatically shut down. Within minutes fireman arrived on the 8th floor speaking to us through the door several feet above us and via the elevator phone. It would take about twenty minutes to move the cables manually, move the car into position to retrieve us, and assuring us we were in no danger.

The firemen suggested we sit on the floor and relax until they could get us out. Relax! Every fear that had lingered for years, the ediginess felt each time I rode an elevator raced through me. The nightmare of millions was mine, inside a metal 6x6x10 foot box suspended seven stories above street level, held by mere cables, inside a burning building, I sat down with a sob of fear.

My male co-workers sat on the floor and calmly talked work stuff while I sat frozen in place on the floor, my head lying on my arms across my knees. I had only one choice, pray while my nerves and body shivered and shook. Thirty minutes later the slow, groaning car moved to the 7th floor, the doors manually opened by smiling fireman who took our hands as we stepped out, said we were in no danger, then guided us down the stairwell and outside.

The fire was quickly contained on an upper floor, but the building and street area would be closed. After an EMT checked us over the firemen told the three of us to go home. I don't remember the drive out of the city, my mind so scattered, and my brain numb, I'm sure I drove like a robot. To no one's surprise I quickly changed jobs, vowing never to work in a building more than four stories high.

Over time I learned there was an entire group of elevator passengers who had at one time found themselves stuck between floors in a broken elevator or in one in a burning building. Some were odd experiences, a few very scary, others comical, all worth retelling. Several "victims" vowed to never board an elevator again while others shrugged off their scary experience as just another day.

Elevator stories heard over the years from people who had experienced ordeals ranging from getting stuck between floors to people fussing and fighting, arguing, insulting each other, lawyers yelling at clients, to mothers with ill-behaved children. The funniest stories were those depicting smells endured, everything from diaper stink, unwashed bodies, overwhelming lunch smells, and strong after-shave and perfumes. The most common, and worse, the smell rarely spoken of; the take-your-breath-away release of ill wind by gassy riders.

If we give it thought, movie-makers should be blamed for feeding our fear of elevators. Scenes of killing people with guns, knives, poison gas, or beating passengers up, robbing and kidnapping. The worst, sabotaging the elevator where it breaks loose and crashes in an explosion on the bottom floor. See what I mean.

However, a pet peeve traveling in Europe was the lack of elevators. I'm not kidding here. There are at least fifty-billion stairs to climb if you plan to visit historical sites, museums, or art galleries almost anywhere in Europe. Half are uneven or broken medieval stone steps, which might be Europe's take on exercise, or their enjoyment of watching tourists climbing, falling, and stumbling across the continent.

In my youthful travels in Europe, two full days were spent in the Louvre Museum because, one it is nearly the size of Delaware, two, it had no elevator at that time, or if they did it was broken or hidden away in some dark basement. This encouraged visiting other floors via 1,680 stair steps! But the real challenge came throughout Great Britain, Italy, France, and Greece where I swear, I climbed at least 100,000 steps to see some of the world's greatest sites, museums, and treasures.

I was exhausted because not one elevator had been installed in places I traveled. Although, there was (is) an elevator in the Eiffel Tower. Which is where I discovered, while stuffed in a 4 ft x 4 ft box against thirty tourists, arm deodorant is not a commonly used product by many. This was the main reason I choose not to take the elevator to leave the magnificent aerial sights of Paris. I choose instead to take the stairs; all 1,665 of them back down the inside of the tower.

Argue with me, say elevators are newer, safer, high tech, sleek, and glide along effortlessly without concern. Well, sometimes new things are made to look better than they are. My prediction? Everything new or old will at some point break, elevators will always be suspect, scare us on occasion, and continue to urge us to take the stairs.

Laziness

One might assume occasional complaining about work gives the impression a person might be a bit lazy. Being a sporadic slacker doesn't mean one is shiftless, however, I do admit to grumbling about work sometimes, which isn't exactly laziness. I'm simply voicing displeasure over certain drudgery if it interferes with my pleasurable or idle time. Still, I don't consider myself a do-nothing type person for I've been working practically all my life.

As a youth my parents assigned chores to each of their children based on their age, giving instructions and guided them in dos and don'ts. If a job wasn't done right it would result in the task needing to be done over, so the goal was to learn to do it right. If a task was poorly done or not finished on a timely basis, it had to be done over. So, doing a job right the first time was a great motivator as I certainly didn't want to do it twice. That too might be considered a type of laziness.

Only lazy people were slack in their work, left property unkempt, or a home untidy; it bred mischief and incompetence, my parents preached. Working to keep one's home and property neat and well working was the sign of a good citizen, caring, and solid. Working during early years and on through teen years was expected; it built character and responsibility, according to my parents. Just as important, the reward from work was money to spend and save for things wanted and needed.

My parents also pointed out during those early working years, finding a job or career that suited you would give you joy and status, a place in the world. The biggest motivator was of course money. So early on the search for a career that would keep one working with a good income was always the goal.

However, to keep up with wants and needs, time spent at work sometimes flowed into weekends and nights, mostly to get the job done and of course extra pay. Unfortunately, this grinding schedule left little time for play and pleasure. Still we keep busy, hard at work, proud of our accomplishments but grumble when it never lets up. This doesn't mean one is lazy for grumbling over long hours of work, it simply means idleness seems a more pleasant idea.

In retirement years, I personally find the drudgery of doing much of anything resembling work a drag on my pleasure time. But I'm not shiftless, I'm just tired of working, so I often whine about tasks around the home that must be done. This may sound lackadaisical, despite the fact I'm usually rather ambitious. However, there are days when I simply don't want to do anything, mostly because I enjoy pleasure time and loafing.

This sometimes means housework is delayed for as long as possible, I don't like cleaning ashes from the fireplace, it makes me cough, and dusting sends me into a sneezing fit, so I dally about doing these jobs. Pulling weeds from flower beds seems a useless chore, they grow right back, and I absolutely detest grocery shopping. Loading and unloading a cart, carrying items to the house, unpacking it all, and putting everything away, it's just plain work.

This type behavior and attitude hints at laziness, no doubt about it, but there are certain undertakings which should be put off for as long as possible in hopes someone else will take them on. Unfortunately, it seems more and more younger people have adopted this same attitude, expecting someone else to do the job they should be doing. This could possibly be construed as downright lazy, or possibly imply they are complete dawdlers.

Although, consider this. Have you looked closely at our highways and streets lately? They are continually strewn with trash. This proves that some of the people driving could be deemed the laziest on the planet by choosing to throw trash along the roadways instead of putting it where it belongs. Well, think about it! When was the last time you drove any highway and found it free of trash? See what I mean, therein gives credibility to this, some drivers are lazy.

I'm something of an optimistic doubter for I have great hope for those doing work needed and doubt the busy generation will take time for pleasure or lounging about. Step away, sit quietly reading a good book, take time out to play sports or kick back and watch sports on the television. Best, take time for a trip, a vacation wanted and needed. Or find the bliss in disappearing for a nap, a walk on the beach or in the woods, downtime from work and an overloaded mind, which I don't consider laziness.

A famous spiritual leader once said a true happiness in life is to know a job has been well done but casual loitering is good for the soul and random rest is marvelous. Consider too; the saying cleanliness is next to Godliness might move one to believe laziness could possibly be next to mischievousness, even incompetence.

But hey, carefree dawdling is sheer bliss and piddlin' should be practiced often, considered a cultural tradition. It's quite possible our brain and body enjoy the down time of resting and relaxing, take pride in putting aside tasks of the daily grind and simply bask in the plan of getting the most out of life every day.

Biography of Carol Cook

Carol is the author of five books of short stories and essays and five books of poetry. She is a member of the Authors Guild, the Texas Marketing Guild, and the Poetry Society of Texas. Writing since her youth, Carol wrote during the years of young motherhood raising children, working for a living wage, and now in retirement. She honed her writing skills at Community Colleges, in night schools, and writing classes, never earning a degree in anything. Her hilariously laugh out loud stories have been published in newspapers and magazines for years, gaining a fan club who enjoyed her humorous and cranky opinions. For decades she has poked fun at those wandering aimlessly through life, at herself, and those who experienced man kinds outlandish misdeeds in stupidity, publishing her take on these mysteries of life. She asks how and why intelligent people are getting lost in familiar places and why our government officials are lying to us continuously. Her edgy voice has questioned and scolded, outlined ridiculous behavior, and given us insights on promises made, phobias, surprises, and the misadventures the general public indulge in. Carol captures everyday life, daily frustrations, dishes on medical maladies, relatives, the food we eat, and asks, "What's with the fake meat crap". She wonders why so many are lacking in commonsense as they stagger across the world, why are the masses so wasteful, and what happened to manners?

Carol and her husband internationally accredited watercolor artist, Robert W. Cook live in Texas beside a lake with their two Maltese dogs, Sugar and Spice.

Contact Carol: **carolbcook@metro411.net**

https://www.carolcookwriter.com

Acknowledgements

My sincere thanks to Tracy Traynor of With a Flourish and a Polish Editing, your help with correcting my typo's and grammar errors went beyond the call of duty, bless you!

And to Bayley Gonzales, Graphic Artist at Print One Granbury who helped me create the cover for this book and helped make the layout perfect, thank you for your patience and talent.

Carol Cook: https://carolcookwriter.com

Tracy Traynor: https://flourishandapolish.wordpress.com

Print One: www.printonegranbury.com

Artisans Book Reviews: www.artisansbookreviews.com

Other Humor Books by Carol

Why Didn't Someone Tell Me?   What Happened?

That Can't Be Right!   You're Kidding?

Book Reviews

I Can't Believe this! By Carol Cook offers a fresh commentary about the people and situations that we encounter and struggle with on a daily basis. From the ridiculous (the Aluminum Foil Crisis) to the sublime (the trend for designer luggage), Carol Cook roasts it all with her unique tongue-in cheek delivery.

The tone for this collection of essays is set from the start, with the quote from Voltaire – "Commonsense isn't common" and it sure is fun to read about the lack of it! In addition to bemoaning burning issues, such as the death of manners, Carol Cook has written a collection that includes reminiscences from her childhood, my favorites being her wonderful ode to the turkey sandwich and why we should all be cooking with lard. She's not afraid to get personal, as she tells of her struggles dealing with "sparkalaphobia" and how memory loss can be liberating. And last but not least, author Carol Cook's opinion pieces will give you a fresh perspective on the foibles of how the human races, such as the media's attempt to create an aluminum foil crisis and the need to throw the book at criminals who had the gall to attempt a "grand theft avocado".

Aside from the gentle humor of the stories, what I appreciated the most about these vignettes of everyday life was the sense of the familiar. I felt like I could have been sitting on the porch having sweet tea and conversation with my feisty Aunt, as she was telling me about the latest neighborhood gossip or nonsense she heard on the television. As I was reading, I often found myself smiling and agreeing that I, too, hate mosquitoes with every fiber of my being and that "fake food" shouldn't be a thing. It was refreshing to lose myself in a book that pointed out how ridiculous, yet wonderful, life can be.

I Can't Believe this! By Carol Cook is an entertaining series of snapshots that give us the opportunity to laugh at ourselves and the craziness around us. If you're a fan of humorists like Erma Bombeck or Dave Barry, you'll enjoy this light-hearted book!

Artisan Book Reviews   **www.artisanbookreviews.com**